Fresh Leaves

Short Stories

By

New Writers

First published in 2018 by

Vineleaves Publishing

Copyright © 2018 Vineleaves Publishing

ISBN:

Edited by C J Mitchell

Typeset in 11pt minion pro by

www.vineleavespublishing.co.uk

Printed and bound by ingram spark

*For the Creative Writing
Lectures at the Univeristy of
Gloucestershire*

IV

Contents

VIII

Henry's Seagull

By
Carol Hilton

The seagull made a second pass, hovered mid-air, then- decision made, landed on the patio table. The sudden invasion made Henry jerk his mug; splashing pale tea onto the photo. The gull tilted its neck legs slightly astride like a feathered pirate surveying its plunder.

Henry snatched the photo up, pulled out a crumpled hanky from his pocket, and blotted it as tenderly as if it was a new born.

'Give you a fright?' A female voice said. The spiky-haired café assistant had rushed up to Henry, cloth in hand.

The seagull lunged towards the white plate and trans-fixed Henry with its pale-yellow eyes before dipping its neck and spearing a chunk of his panini.

'Shoo.' Mia flapped her cloth.

The seagull ignored her. It stared back brazen, resolute.

'Any damage?' She nodded to his photo as she edged round the table mopping up the puddle while keeping one eye on the bird.

Henry glanced at the photo and shook his head.

'Someone special?' she tried again.

Henry's eyes crinkled as he attempted a smile. 'Mmm, was all he could manage.' He tucked the stained photo back in his tweed jacket.

He shouldn't have returned. He regretted even entering the café. So overjoyed to find it in the same row of shops, the original 'Falcone' sign in the window he'd impulsively pushed open the door, his mouth savouring the aroma of home-made Biscotti, pastries and cakes, and ordered lunch. Looking around, he noticed some familiar misshapen almond-scented cakes. 'Bruttiboni,' he whispered reverently.

The assistant had looked up from her order pad. 'Want one for afters?'

Henry had felt the hairs prickle on his neck. Gina had told him about Bruttiboni in this very café. But that was over thirty years ago. This girl hadn't even been born then. He looked at the assistant. Under her black hair and rather alarming eyebrow piercing, she had familiar lively brown eyes, wide mouth and smooth honey skin.

The memory was so unexpected and unbearably painful that it was all Henry could do to mutely shake his head when she'd pointed at the cakes. He had picked up his tray and knocking into empty chairs shuffled through the French doors to the empty patio. Sinking down, before his trembling legs gave way, he had peered back inside the café. Originally an ice cream parlour, the café had been *the* place for the Brighton youth. But now red vinyl booths had given way to bistro tables and driftwood sculptures. Reassured to spot the original black and white floor tiles, Henry had leant forward to take a sip of tea, just as the seagull had attacked. The seagull flapped upwards to the patio lamppost. Replete, a string of mozzarella swung like a lizard's tail from one side of its beak. Henry surveyed his ravaged lunch then picked up his coat.

The assistant put out a hand to stop him. 'Hey, I'll make another panini.' She picked up his mug. 'On the house.'

'Oh no, that won't be…I'm fine.' Henry glanced towards the door.

'Course I will. Your cheeky friend has ruined yours.' Mia said. 'Please?' She bustled away before he could refuse.

'Most kind,' he said, inwardly cursing his unfailing politeness. He watched as she switched on the grill and then disappeared through a door marked 'Staff Only.'

The café fell silent apart from the ticking oven clock. He could hear an urgent conversation emerging from behind the staff door.

On the lamppost, the seagull half-raised its wings to peck at his feathers. As Henry watched, he felt a thrill of connection to something wild and free: a maverick, sizzling with energy and impatient for adventure.

Gina had been working here, in her father's café when they'd first met. Henry had spent much of that summer perched on a barstool admiring her, wearing his University scarf secretly hoping that he exuded an aura of sophistication. Perhaps it had. One afternoon Gina had placed a piece of Bruttiboni in front of him.

'Do you know what Bruttiboni means in English?' She'd asked. That summer they'd become inseparable. His suitcase had never felt so heavy when he'd returned to Cambridge in September.

'How's your seagull?' Mia interrupted his thoughts and placed a mug down. 'Panini's nearly done.' She glanced at the closed staff door.

'Most kind.' Henry picked up a sugar sachet.

'Well, thought you needed it,' she paused. 'You looked, like….' she bit her lip.

'What?' asked Henry.

'Lonely, you know?' she said.

'Goodness me,' he coughed. He worked his mouth into a twisted smile to reassure her. 'No, sorry, I'm fine. Really.'

Her eyes narrowed as she stared at him.

Henry shifted uneasily. 'Honestly.' He gently shook the sachet. 'I retired this summer, and I'm just getting used...'

Before he could continue Mia's phone in her back pocket whirred. She gave him an apologetic look she reluctantly turned away to mutter some rapid-fire Italianinto it.

Henry's shoulders slumped as he recalled his retirement 'do' earlier that year. In his imagination he'd always imagined his final day as a teacher would consist of admiring speeches and tearful students. Instead, he'd shifted uncomfortably in the staff room on a stifling June afternoon listening to a mumbled speech by the "Team Leader." Henry's quiet response had been punctuated by the loud clinking of keys and rustling bags as his colleagues glanced furtively at the clock. By the time Henry had emptied his locker, he'd found himself in an almost deserted car park.

He hadn't expected anyone to keep in touch once he retired. Frustratingly it hadn't meant to be that way when he found his first job as History teacher at a shiny new Comprehensive. In those days he'd have laughed at the thought that he would end up spending his whole career there. Gradually becoming disillusioned by school politics, angry parents, and the unruly students. His life might not have been this way if his mother hadn't taken ill.

It was just before his very first Christmas break when Henry heard a tap on the classroom door. The school secretary. His mother had been taken to hospital having taken a fall in Tesco's. Henry found her, a small doll tucked in the large industrial sized bed, slightly shaken and puzzled by her "dizzy spell." A discussion with specialists revealed the early stages of MS. As his father had died when he was young in a meaningless hot war, Henry had taken charge, vowing to care for her.

Henry had been fifty-six when his mother died. After the funeral he'd sat at the scrubbed table, head bowed, cradling her reading glasses. It had grown dark by the time he shuffled out to the garden. In the velvet shadows, he could almost hear her gentle voice reminding him to give the herbs a good soaking. It was only the following morning when Henry realised that he'd prepared two mugs of tea that he slumped on the floor crying like a schoolboy.

The next week Henry had returned to school ready to deliver his lesson on the downfall of the Roman Empire with the infamous 9c. He entered the classroom with blank eyes and a set jaw, determined to carry on. But by lunchtime rumours had gone around the school that the normally mild Mr Wheater had "cracked." Varied reports of marker pens and staplers being thrown across the room had found their way to the staff room. After school Henry had been found in the stationary cupboard staring sight-lessly at the shelves marked Highlighters. That summer he retired on medical grounds.

After the ignominious end of his teaching career, Henry wandered listlessly around the house staring sightlessly out the window until the falling leaves invaded his garden forcing him to sweep them up. The cool air roused Henry to clear the rooms, a fresh start. While picking up an armful of old maps, Gina's photo had fallen out. He'd picked it up, his mind a kaleidoscope of memories. 'Henry and Gina forever,' still visible in Gina's loopy handwriting inscribed on the back. Forever. How naive they were to make plans: travel, marry, children. Henry had been saving for an engagement ring for Gina's Christmas present when he found out about his mother's condition. His dreams had evaporated as swiftly as the morning sea mist. Henry had decided they must part; for Gina's sake. He knew she'd refuse to break up, insist on helping with his mother. He couldn't let her do that, end up trapped. He lay awake all night then, a decision made, asked her to meet him at the wind shelter on the pier.

'There's someone else.' He'd started, hesitant as he stumbled through his prepared script. As he spun his lies, his stomach felt like lead.

Gina rounded on him with a barrage of questions.

'Susan.' 'Teaches P.E.' 'Yes, it's serious.' He'd mumbled.

He hung his head to avoid her tears, only raising it when he heard her walk away, the salt spray glistening on her hair. Below him the crashing sea threw itself relentlessly against the pier legs; at that moment he wanted the whole structure to collapse into the broiling froth and take him with it.

Gina hadn't remained long in Brighton after their break-up. Henry had heard through their neighbour that Gina had flown to her Sicilian grandparents and a suitable cousin had been found for her.

Their neighbour, Enid had sniffed loudly. 'She's running his business. Shoe factory or handbags?' She blew on her tea. 'Apparently, she's the size of a house what with expecting twins. Poor girl.'

Henry had gagged as some acid rushed into his mouth. He stared out the window at the purple Dahlias. He realised that he hated Dahlias.

Over the years Henry, busy with work and his mother had never tried to contact Gina. But somehow the forgotten photo prompted him. He'd propped it up on his mantelpiece and stared at it each night. He pulled a face at his younger self, hair neatly trimmed, shirt and tie. What a pompous ass he'd looked in those days. His arm was slung casually round a flushed-looking Gina. Her long tangled black hair framed her dusky complexion and almost too-wide mouth, reminding Henry of a young Sophia Loren. They had just got off the dodgems. Henry could still hear the klaxons, the hot oily smell of the bumper cars and Gina's warm body snuggled up tight to him. He shook his head to shut out the juke-box of memories that played through his mind.

Perhaps he had made the wrong decision; maybe they could have made it work? Too late now. But still, he felt an overwhelming urge to return to the café. Just one visit.

The grill pinged and, Mia rapped her knuckles loudly on the staff door.

Puzzled Henry looked up. The door opened slowly. Henry couldn't breathe.

It was Gina. Her black hair speckled with fine threads of white was neatly tied back. Even with fine wrinkles and looking worryingly thin, it was still his lovely Gina.

Henry tried to speak but croaked instead.

Gina picked up the Panini and walked towards him, a flash of recognition in her eyes betrayed her insouciance. Her simple black dress swirled around her still sensational legs as she stepped onto the patio.

'Your Panini.' She banged the plate on the table, startling both Henry and the seagull.

Henry half rose uncertainly.

Gina sat down opposite Henry and pointed at the photo. 'May I?'

Henry handed it across.

Gina tapped at the photo. 'Stupid.' Her husky voice trembled. 'Why do you carry that? What happened to Susan? Marry her?' Tossing the photo back, she crossed her arms.

'Susan? I didn't….' Henry paused. How could he explain?

'What?' Her eyes flashed.

'There's been no-one. I never married.'

Gina relaxed and sat back in her seat. 'So why are you here? Why now?'

'Trip down memory lane.' He still couldn't believe she was sitting in front of him. 'Don't you live in Italy?'

'I'm visiting Mia my youngest. It's her café now.' She smiled. 'She looks like me, no?'

Henry nodded. 'Were you happy Gina?' He had to know.

'Happy?' Gina shrugged. 'He was no…Prince Charming, but I have my children, the business. Now,' she picked up Henry's knife and polished it, '…I'm alone again.'

Henry slowly shook his head. 'You haven't changed. Still beautiful.' The words tumbled out.

Gina tucked a stray hair behind her ear. 'Liar. I'm the Bride of Frankenstein these days.' Absentmindedly she chopped the Panini into quarters, before waving the knife accusingly at him. 'You haven't aged. Not one bit.'

Henry swallowed. 'Gina, I'm sorry about … '

Gina held up a finger. 'No. The past is past.'

She frowned at Henry's congealed Panini, scraped her chair back and walked over to the counter.

Uncertain Henry stood and picked up his raincoat.

'Hey.' Gina shouted across, 'Where are you going? I'm getting us some Bruttiboni.' she gave him a wide smile.

'You used to adore it. No?'

As Henry drew near to take a plate, her hand touched his. A sign of forgiveness. A sign of promise.

Henry's gull, spotting the unguarded Panini and gleefully dived down for a piece before taking flight. Avoiding its feathered pursuers, it soared over rooftops before finding a perch near a smaller gull who shuffled sideways to make room.

Henry smiled. They'd both come home.

Letting Go

By
Claire Harrison

It was a fine afternoon on Sycamore Road. I hardly noticed the Cherry Blossom trees that lined the street as I pulled into our driveway that Monday afternoon. I sat for a moment watching the digital clock. One more minute and I'd get out. I could see the front door was open, but from this angle, I couldn't see my husband's feet. I'd see them once I got out of the car. I knew they were there because Jenny, my next-door neighbour, had called me.

'You need to come home,' she'd said. 'Something's wrong; I think Matthew's collapsed, I can see his feet by the front door.'

Jenny's head was peeking from behind the box hedge that separated our two houses. She wasn't very tall; she must have been standing on tiptoe, her head bobbed up and down as she lost her balance.

I took a deep breath and stepped out of the car. 'Everything alright?' Jenny shouted.

'Yes,' I waved. 'I'm sure everything's fine.' Jenny looked unconvinced. 'I've rung the police,' she said. 'Just in case. I didn't want to go in… you never know….'

Jenny was a member of the Neighbourhood Watch. I'd left my mobile phone number and spare key with her once when we went away.

'That's kind, thank you,' I said. 'I'm sure they won't be necessary. As I walked towards the front door, I could see Matthew's ankles, and size 10's resting neatly on the doorstep. I took a breath, pushed the door wide open and stepped over his legs. He was supine, on the floor, his left calf touching the leg of the hall table. His head lay between the staircase and the sitting room door. I put my keys down on the table and bent down towards him.

'Matthew, get up.' I gently nudged his arm with my hand. No response. I pushed a little harder, then leaned in closer to get a better view of his chest. It was moving, so he was breathing.

I stepped over his head, walked through to the kitchen and dialled the Doctor's. The surgery was just across the road from the house.

This wasn't the first time he'd collapsed. During the pat six months, he'd passed out in Sainsburys, over Risotto Al Funghi at Carluccio's, and in the middle of my parents' anniversary dinner. Each time he'd been taken to the hospital, and each time they couldn't find anything wrong. Stress they said causes all sorts of problems; panic attacks, pseudo heart attacks, general pain in the arse attacks. I was trying to be understanding, but these "attacks" always seem to happen at the most inconvenient moment.

As I sat, phone in hand, waiting for my call to be answered, I looked across to the kitchen window. Matthew had come home for lunch; a dirty plate sat in the sink, breadcrumbs and a knife on the breadboard. Why would he leave work, a 30-minute drive, to eat lunch at home on his own?

Finally, the receptionist answered. 'Hello,' I said. 'This is Karen James from No 24, across the road. My husband has collapsed in the hallway, and I need a Doctor… no, he can't come into the surgery, he's lying on the floor, I can't get the front door closed. I think it's probably a panic attack…yes, he's breathing. Yes… we're right opposite; the Doctor won't need to drive, it's a two-minute walk. OK, thank you.'

Matthew groaned slightly. I put the phone down, stepped over him into the sitting room and picked up one of the cushions and the plaid throw off the sofa. Lifting his head, I placed it underneath and then stretched out the throw over his body. The spring sunshine at the front of the house touched Matthew's feet, but there was still a chill in the air. I pulled the front door open a little more so I could hear when the Doctor arrived and sat on the bottom stair.

It was strangely peaceful. The only sound was the ticking of the big clock which hung on the wall, behind the front door. We'd bought it because it looked a little like the clock in Paddington Station, where Matthew and I first met. We'd been waiting for the same train, 6.30pm to Swindon, it was delayed. The station's coffee shop was rammed, with just one free table, and we ended up sitting next to each other while we waited.

'Do you mind?' he had asked as he gestured at the seat next to mine.

I shook my head. 'Not at all.'

He looked sort of homely, slightly rumpled from a day in the city. He was carrying a large portfolio case in one hand and holding an old rucksack in the other. It was covered in badges and handwriting and bits of stapled cloth; it looked like a piece of modern art.

'I love your rucksack,' I said. He told me it was a mobile memento of the people he'd met, the places he'd been, and each mark told a story. And that's how it all started, over a coffee at Paddington Station.

Here we were, eight years later, Matthew lying on the hall floor and me sitting on the bottom step, waiting for the doctor. The last few times he'd collapsed we'd been surrounded by people who'd taken charge, but this time I was on my own. This time it was down to me, and I didn't know how to make it right. I looked at Matthew, really looked at him. I no longer knew how I felt about this person lying on the floor. I didn't recognise this man that suffered from panic attacks. This man who'd once travelled the world alone with his crazy rucksack. I'd fallen in love with a free spirit, a photographer who had the ability to wring every moment out of life and turn it into a memory.

As we waited in that coffee shop all those years ago, I had looked through his portfolio; swathes of orange, pink and emerald silk wrapped around Indian women as they sat on the steps in a local market. I could almost hear the jangle of their gold bangles as they talked. An old man, playing cards in a remote French village, a Gauloises dripped from his mouth, his face, a road map of a life well lived, his eyes still sparkled, the flame not yet extinguished. But amongst the vibrant, living colours, one image stood out. A young child sat on a filthy, grey, ripped sofa surrounded by black mountains of rubbish. Her yellow vest the only colour across the wasteland, a Primrose in a slag heap. Her feet and face were filthy, her grubby shoes neatly placed side by side, next to the sofa, as if at home, not wanting to get it dirty. This was her life; it had no colour.

The crunch of feet on gravel told me the Doctor had arrived. I stood up as she stepped over Matthew. 'Hello, I'm Doctor Stevenson… and this is Matthew?'

'Yes.'

'How long has he been like this?'

'I'm not sure, I came home about 10 minutes ago, my next-door neighbour called me, she'd noticed the front door open… he's done this before.'

She bent down and did the usual checks, pulse, heart, blood pressure. 'I can't find anything immediately wrong, but he should get thoroughly checked out. I'll call an ambulance.' She walked outside and took out her mobile phone.

Matthew moaned again. I wanted to tell him everything would be OK, but I couldn't. Instead, I knelt down and touched his arm. 'Matthew, the ambulance is on its way. It won't be long.'

Sycamore Road became a busy place that afternoon. The ambulance arrived followed by a police car, an opera of professional voices and decisions. Matthew was examined and lifted into the ambulance and all along the police radio voiced a commentary in the background. Doors slammed, and gravel grumbled. Then, finally, it was silent again. I stood in the doorway for a moment and watched the blossoms fall gently onto the pavement.

I said I'd follow the ambulance. I needed to call Matthew's parents and tell work I wouldn't be back that afternoon. As I closed the front door I noticed Matthew's keys, he must have had them in his hand as he was leaving to go back to work. They'd slid across the floor and nestled in the corner, between the staircase and the skirting board. I picked them up, and ran my thumb over the keyring. It was one of those clear, cheap plastic ones with a photo inside. I'd bought it as a silly gift after we got engaged. The photo was one of Matthew's, the old Frenchman with that sparkle in his eyes and on the back I'd written 'yours forever, may the fire never go out'.

It was as if the Frenchman's cigarette had burnt my hand, but I couldn't let go. I clenched the keyring tighter, feeling the pain searing into my skin. I wanted it to hurt, because it was all my fault. For years I'd studied to become a lawyer and Matthew had supported me. He'd given up his dreams to help me find mine. His travels of discovery had turned into a drab job, skittles on a Tuesday night and take away Fridays. His life had no colour because I'd taken away his future.

I dropped the keys onto the hall table and walked upstairs. The rucksack sat in a storage box at the back of the wardrobe in the spare bedroom. I lifted the box onto the bed and took the rucksack out. I ran my hand over the badges and bits of cloth and slowly opened the zip. Inside were a handful of photos, smiling faces laughing up at me. I grabbed the bag and stood up, walking over those faces as they fell to the floor. I stumbled into our bedroom and opened drawers, snatching at socks, jumpers, jeans, stuffing clothes into the rucksack until it was full. In the bathroom, I took Matthew's toothbrush and shaving kit from the cabinet and put them in the front pocket. I ran down the stairs, picked up my keys and slammed the front door behind me.

'Everything alright?' Jenny's voice slithered across the box hedge. Ignoring her, I jumped into the car and sped down Sycamore Road towards the hospital. There was something I needed to do first.

Matthew was hooked up to a heart monitor. His eyes closed, and he looked exhausted. I walked towards his bed and gently touched his arm.

He opened his eyes. 'Hello, you. I'm sorry,' he said quietly. 'This is turning into a habit.'

'Don't be silly,' I said, sitting on the side of the bed. 'How're you feeling?'

'Like I could sleep for a week. This is all pointless,' Matthew said gesturing towards the monitor. 'I'm just wasting everyone's time.' He sat himself up in the bed and caught sight of the rucksack on the floor. 'What's that doing....'

'Matthew, why did you come home for lunch today?' He looked at me for a moment, then lowered his head slightly. For a few seconds, we sat in silence.

'I didn't want to go back...I can't stand it anymore,' he said. 'I feel like I'm walking on a tightrope. I'm trying so hard to keep my balance, yet all I want to do is jump off... I'm sorry, I know that sounds stupid.' He couldn't look at me and turned his gaze towards the rucksack. His words opened up the space between us, and I knew the decision I'd made earlier that day was right.

'I'm the one who's sorry.'

Matthew turned his head towards me. 'You need your life back,' I said. 'I didn't mean to; I didn't realise….I was so caught up in….' my voice waivered, and Matthew held my hand.

'You didn't take it,' he said gently. 'I gave it to you. I don't want a life without you.'

I picked up the rucksack and put it at the foot of his bed.

He looked up at me. 'What does that mean?' he asked.

'I want you to be happy… I want to see the fire in your eyes when you talk about the places you've been and the people you've met. I want you back.'

I undid the zip on the rucksack and took out a little box which I gave to him. Inside was a key ring, not cheap and plastic but solid silver, made to last, I'd had it engraved on the way to the hospital, it said 'yours forever, no matter how far apart'.

The Sheep's Skin

By
Rosie James

It's pouring with rain by the time that Niamh reaches the border that separates the Republic of Ireland from the North. Water trickles down the back of her neck, soaking her right to the skin, and making her clammy. Niamh steps from one foot to the other. There are a few people in front of her, looking wet and miserable. The border guards look miserable too, in their soggy uniforms. Niamh would feel sorry for them if they weren't British. Her passport is in her rucksack, slung over the handlebars of her bike, an FT Team replica that used to be her brothers. She has to hold onto her bike with one hand, pushing it forward when the queue moves an inch every five minutes or so. The rucksack itself is the colour of dried blood, made of scratchy canvas, but it's the only one Niamh has. She's trying not to look suspicious, even though at this moment in time, she has nothing to hide. The rucksack is just a rucksack, empty, like her sister.

'Name?' The Garda barks and makes Niamh jump. He's in his 30's, with a clipped British accent. There's something in his eyes too, something that Niamh doesn't like.

'Niamh,' she says, 'Niamh Byrne.'

'How old are you?'

Niamh opens her mouth to answer but is interrupted by a sudden blast of radio music coming from the guard station. It's pouring out from the loudspeaker that screeches orders at the waiting people and cars. Niamh and the Garda turned to see a younger soldier standing there, looking guilty as the first chords of *Cosmic Dancer*, by T-Rex sounded in the air.

'Turn that bloody racket down!' The Garda roars, and other soldier fumbles to turn it off, the loudspeaker spluttering. 'You're a soldier, not a DJ!'

Niamh's heard the song played in snatches from her brother's radio, and opens her rucksack to rescue her passport. It's going to get damp in the rain, and Niamh just prays it won't ruin it. She could have gotten a fake passport, they're easy enough to make, but she was too afraid.

The Garda turns back to her once the radio has been switched off and snatches her passport. He rolls his eyes when he flicks through it.

'Gaelic again,' he says, pronouncing the word 'Gaelic' like a swear word.

He opens the passport to the page where her photograph is stuck in and examines her details.

'You're eighteen?' He asks, and Niamh nods.

'Yes.'

'And why are you crossing the border today?'

'I'm meeting a friend,' Niamh says, the lie falters a little on her tongue.

'How did you make friends with someone on this side of the border?'

'We went to school together.' Niamh lies, 'Her Da moved when he got a new job.'

The Garda stares her down for a moment and then holds out his hand. 'Bag.'

Niamh offers him her rucksack, and he tips it out onto the ground. There's not much inside it anyway, her purse, a packet of tissues, and a bottle of water. The items bounce on the pavement, and the guard nudges them with his foot.

What's your friend's name?'

'Mary.' Niamh lies, and he looks at her for a very long moment. Niamh looks back at him. Her mother always says that Nimah has a queer stare, that there's something not right about her.

Finally, he looks away. 'Collect your things.' He says, 'Welcome to Northern Ireland.'

'Thank you.' Niamh bends down to collect her belongings, still not looking at the guard. She can feel sweat trickling down her back. 'Have a nice day.'

The Garda doesn't reply.

The pub is so close to the border that Niamh wonders why the British haven't knocked it down yet. It's called The Squealing Pig, and there's a sign hanging above the door of a pig about to get axed by a farmer. The pig has a St George's flag pin clipped to its ear, and Niamh gazes at it for a moment, before tying her bicycle to the railings outside. It's quiet inside the pub. Nimah hopes it isn't an omen, and something was not about to go wrong.

It was her sister, Siobhán that put her up to this. It's for the greater good; she'd said, laying on Niamh's bed and staring up at the ceiling. Siobhan had been acting differently ever since she got back from the baby home. She didn't even like Niamh to hug her anymore; she was cold and quiet. She'd got involved with 'some people'. That was all that she would tell Niamh as she lay on her bed, one hand on her still bloated stomach. She'd told Niamh that by smuggling, Niamh was doing the whole Republic a favour.

There was only a couple of people in the pub. Men, dotted around the place on separate tables, staring into their pint glasses. One of them notices her and lumbers to his feet like an angry bear.

'What's your name?' He asks, towering over her, Niamh has to strain to look at him.

'Niamh,' she says, knowing the way she pronounces it shows she's from the Republic. There's a long moment of silence. Niamh wonders if he's going to throw her out of the pub, she wouldn't be surprised. Instead, he looks her up and down, and then relaxes.

'You're alright,' he says. Niamh stares at him.

He turns back to his table, and Niamh wonders if he's actually alright in the head. The man sits down, grunting as he gets himself settled. Niamh looks around the pub, but the men are plainly ignoring her. Niamh collects herself and moves towards the bar. There's the clattering of glass from the bar. Someone is standing on a stool putting bottles and glasses away on the shelves behind. Niamh moves closer, hoping they'll be able to help her. The bartender jumps down off the stool and turns to face Niamh. It's a girl, with black cropped hair, and heavy black eyeliner. She looks Niamh up and down, and Niamh tilts her chin up.

'What do you want?' The girl asks. She has a strong Northern accent. 'I'm not serving if you don't have any money.'

'I…' Niamh says, fiddling with her bag. 'My sister sent me.'

'Oh shit.' The girl says. Something in the girl's face has softened, and Niamh wonders how her sister knows this girl. She's one of 'those people', Niamh suspects. 'You're Niamh?'

'Yes,' Niamh says, and the girl offers her hand.

'Maeve,' she replies, and Niamh shakes her hand. 'It's upstairs.'

Maeve steps out from behind the bar and calls across to the man who had accosted Niamh when she first walked in. 'John! Look after bar while I'm gone, alright?'

John lifts up his empty pint glass in reply, and Maeve nods, satisfied. She turns to Niamh and smiles. 'Follow me.'

Maeve manoeuvrers her way through the pub, a fish slipping through water. Niamh traipses after her, feeling like she's a little girl following her sister. She's spent her life trailing after Siobhan, asking her questions. She doesn't feel like she can ask questions anymore.

'Are you sure you're eighteen?' Maeve asks as they're walking up the stairs.

'Yes.' Niamh says, a little stubbornly, 'Why?'

'You just look so little,' she looks over her shoulder with a smile. 'You're a wee babbie.' Niamh must pull a face because Maeve laughs, and continues up the stairs. 'What a face on you!'

'I…' Niamh starts, but Maeve has reached the top of the stairs and has disappeared across a landing. Niamh hurries after her, not wanting to get left behind.

The package is in a bedroom. There are T Rex posters all over the walls, along with Rolling Stones and The Who. Niamh stares at them; her mother would give her all sorts of grief if she put any posters up on her walls, especially if they featured one of these bands. Her mother isn't a fan of pop music or the men in the bands. She thinks they're bad news.

'Here.' Maeve pats the bed. 'Sit down.'

Niamh follows her command, sitting down on the edge of the bed and almost falling off. The bedspread is pink satin, and Niamh gives it a stroke. Maeve pulls back one of the posters of Led Zeppelin to reveal a hole in the wall. Niamh stares as Maeve removes a package wrapped up in brown paper and string, and then deposits it on the bed.Niamh shuffles away from it, and Maeve laughs again.

'They won't bite.' Maeve sits down right next to Niamh. 'They're only condoms.'

Niamh goes a little pink at the word. She's just been referring to them as "the package" in her head, it feels dirty to say what they really are. Condoms. For sex. For a penis. Niamh shudders.

'Have you ever seen a condom before?' Maeve asks.

Niamh shakes her head. She's never had a boyfriend or kissed a boy before. Her parents are both proud of her; she's their good Catholic girl who never does anything out of line. They don't know that she desperately wants to kiss a boy, and she's had dozens of crushes.

'Do you want to see one?' Maeve asks. Her tone is gentle, making Niamh feel even more like a child.

Niamh shakes her head again. Her sister has told her what they look like, balloon-like things of different colours. God doesn't approve of them, or at least, her mother's God doesn't approve of them. Condoms prevent sperm. Which, as her Mum would say, according to God they kill babies. It meant you have to carry the child to full term. Niamh has heard whispers about girls with money who travel to Liverpool to have an abortion. Then there are the girls who try to have abortions in Ireland and end up dead.

'You should be proud of what you're doing, you know,' Maeve says.

'I...' Niamh says. 'They're...'

Maeve looks at her. Niamh fumbles for words. She would do anything for her sister, she loves her with her entire heart, but this, this is different, this is deliberately disobeying God, and her mother, and both of those entities are frightening.

'Are they that important?' Niamh blurts out. 'Really?'

Maeve is silent for a few moments then says. 'Your sister got sent to a baby home, didn't she?'

Niamh nods. 'For sixth months.'

'Do you know what happened there?' Maeve asks.

'No,' Niamh says. Her sister went away pregnant, and came back not-pregnant, with no baby in sight. It was kept hidden for long enough that nobody knew, and now her parents can pretend Sibohan is their virgin daughter and marry her to someone.

'They probably abused her there, told her that she was a sinful, wicked girl, an abomination to God,' Maeve says, and Niamh shakes her head because it's not true. 'But She's not. She goes to church, and she prays with me, and...'

'And do you know what happened to her baby?'

Niamh bites her bottom lip. 'It got adopted?' She asks and crosses herself almost instinctively to pray that she's right. She's always naively assumed that the baby died, and that's why Siobhan was distraught.

'Best case, they removed the baby from her the moment that Siobhan gave birth, and she never got to see it or hold it, or breastfeed it. And then they gave that baby to another couple, and they'll never tell that baby who its true mother is.'

Niamh felt sick.

'Worst case, they forced her into early labour and murdered the child, buried it out in the grounds, where nobody will ever find the body.' Maeve is staring at Niamh so fiercely that Niamh thinks she'll burst into flames. Maeve looks away suddenly though, and Niamh has the feeling there's something she's not telling her. 'And you know, that's most likely what happened.'

'No.' Niamh says, 'You can't murder babies. You'd be evil, and that would be a sin and...'

'Listen to me.' Maeve takes hold of Niamh's hand. 'If you bring those condoms back across the border, you're preventing this. No matter how much you think condoms go against God's will, would you rather condoms? Or dead babies thrown into a pit and left to rot?'

Niamh looks away, as a tear slips out, then another, and then she's crying, and she can't stop. Maeve seems to soften, rubbing Niamh's back.

'It's not fair,' Niamh says, and she realises she's angry, in the pit of her stomach, because that's her *sister* that was hurt. 'It's not fair.'

'I know,' Maeve says, and picks up the package, depositing it on Nimah's lap. 'Which is why you're going to be a brave girl and take these home.'

'How will I get them back across the border?' Niamh asks, and Maeve looks at her with a straight face.

'They're only condoms,' she says innocently, and Niamh wonders if the Garde at the border will laugh at her.

Niamh looks down at the brown package in her lap, the package that is going to stop so many babies from being born. Then she thinks of Siobhan, and her red stretch marks on her stomach, and the way she screams in the night.

'Okay,' she whispers and clenches her fists tight.

Chicken and The Egg

By
Holly Brien

I came home from work to find Rachel slicing a chicken breast. Now, this wouldn't be weird, except for three things. Number one: she's wearing purple tracksuit bottoms. My sister doesn't believe in tracksuit bottoms; she says they are reserved for fat people only. I'm surprised to see her wearing a pair at half six on a Friday evening when she's usually out with Sally; I'm even more surprised she owns a pair at all. Number two: in the three months Rachel has been living in my apartment, not once have I seen her prepare dinner. I cook for her when I get back, and if I'm working late, she will microwave a lasagne. I didn't think she even knew how to turn on the oven. And number three: Rachel is a vegetarian.

'Rach,' I say, dropping my bag on the table. 'What are you doing?'

'Making dinner.' She continues to slice the chicken, not turning around to acknowledge me.

'For who?'

'For us.'

'That's chicken.'

'I thought we'd have a curry tonight.'

'A chicken curry?'

'Yes.'

'*Chicken?*'

'Bloody hell Becky, yes. Chicken.'

I pause, staring at the back of her head, waiting for some sort of explanation. None is offered. 'Rach, you're a vegetarian.'

'Not anymore.'

'Since when?'

'About an hour ago.'

'Why?'

'Fancied a change.'

'You've been vegetarian for 16 years.'

'And now I'm not.'

'But...'

Finally, she turns around. 'I'm trying to concentrate here Becky, do you mind?'

I decide to stop interrogating her for now, so I swallow my questions and try and change the topic.

'So,' I start, walking to the drawer on her left and taking out a knife. I grab a yellow pepper from the side, and after reaching for a chopping board, I begin chopping it into small chunks next to Rachel, who is still working on the chicken. She's struggling to slice it, and I have to stop myself from telling her she's using the wrong knife. Her face is contorted as she grips the cold flesh, wriggling the bread knife side to side. 'How did the appointment go?' I booked Rachel in at the doctor's this morning; she thinks she's had a water infection for the past couple of weeks but has refused to phone them herself. I drove her there during my lunch break. She just shrugs.

'Did they give you anything for it?'

She shrugs again.

'Hopefully something stronger than the ones I picked up in Wilko's.'

She nods.

'Rach, is everything okay?'

That's when she starts crying. No warning, no delicate sniffles signifying she's upset. Just one sudden, hefty roar followed by sobs that cause red tracks to form on her cheeks. Snot dribbles down her top lip and into her mouth, a bubble forming in her nostril and getting bigger and bigger with each jagged breath she takes until it pops. She wipes her nose with the back of her sleeve, and then rubs her eyes, black smudges staining her jumper and her face. I just stare at first, knife hovering over the pepper, my mouth open but no words coming out because I can't think of anything to say. I'm not good when people cry.

When I was 13 and Rachel was 8, we got home from school once to find our mother crying on the living room floor. Her cries were a lot like Rachel's are now. At the time, I didn't know she was crying because my dad had packed his things and ran off to Germany with Mrs Chang's 21-year-old daughter from next door. When we came home to find our mum on the floor that day, all I could think to say was, *'There there,'* while limply rubbing her head in a circular motion.

After about 40 seconds of staring at my sister, the shock wore off, and I decide I should probably do something. I put the knife down and walk to the cupboard, pulling out a half-empty bottle of red wine and take a quick swig before finding glasses and pouring out one for each of us. I then guide Rachel to the chipped, wooden dining table behind us, push my bag and her laptop and a fallen tower of unread mail to the other side, and place the glass in front of her. Her sobs have gotten less aggressive at this point. She looks at the glass and takes a deep breath before gripping it and bringing it to her lips. She tips her head back, about to down it, but then stops herself. Slowly, she puts it down on the table, avoiding my eyes as she pushes it toward me.

Suddenly it clicks.

'Oh, Rach.' I whisper, gently shaking my head. She just stares at the table. 'How far along?'

'3 months.'

'Shit.' I say.

'Yeah.'

'Dylan's?'

'Most likely.'

'Most likely?'

Rachel looks up at me. 'Let's say it's Dylan's, okay?'

'Okay,' I agree. 'You going to tell him?'

'I'd rather eat my own shit after a vindaloo.'

'Right.'

'What am I going to do?'

'We'll figure it out.'

She nods, takes a deep breath. There's a short pause before she speaks again.

'I really hate babies. They're sticky and smelly and ugly, and they look like aliens. I don't want an alien, Becky! I don't want an alien.' Her voice is high.

'Babies are cute.'

'They poop, and they cry, and they vomit, and they make your boobs saggy and your belly saggy and…'

I push my chair back, and jump to her side, turning her around and putting my hands on her shoulder. 'Rachel,' I say, shaking her. 'Breathe.'

'I'm freaking out.'

'I can tell.'

'I don't want a baby.'

'Look,' I say, kneeling down in front of her. 'You know what? I think - I think this is great news.'

'You do?' She looks up at me with bloodshot eyes.

'I do. This is a new chapter of your life. You're bringing something special into this world. We're losing sight of what good news this. You can do this. We can do this.'

I see Rachel take this all in; she's biting her lip, eyebrows furrowed as she subtly nods her head up and down, considering. 'I can do this.' She mutters to herself. The room is silent for a while longer; I can see her eyes flickering as she thinks, her breathing heavy. I stay kneeling, smiling at her, trying to convey that '*this is good news*'. After many stretched out minutes, she finally speaks in a small voice.

'I don't want a baby.'

I take a deep breath. 'Ok,' I say. 'We'll figure it out.'

'Ok.'

Reaching for her hands, I give them a squeeze and smile. Then I let go and clap my own together. 'What do you say we order pizza?'

'But my curry?' She looks back to the discarded meal on the counter.

'Ah. Yes.'

Rachel pauses for a moment. 'How about a burger instead?'

'I'll get the number.'

By the time the food arrives, I've finished both mine and Rachel's glass of wine, and have poured out another. Rachel's been sipping Diet Pepsi instead. The doorbell buzzes during an argument in *Big Brother*. She runs to the door to grab the food, and I get plates from the kitchen, taking them into the front room and placing them on the coffee table. We share out the meals, and I watch as Rachel rips open her double cheeseburger, taking a huge bite. Her eyes close and she moans, chewing slowly and savouring every mouthful.

'This is weird,' I say.

'What?'

'You're eating meat.'

'Mmm Hmm.'

'You've not eaten meat since you were eight.' Her school took them to a farm for a trip in year four and told them about how bacon is made. That night, she went on a hunger strike and tried to get my whole family to turn vegetarian. It lasted about twenty minutes, but from that moment on, she refused to eat meat.

'I know.'

'Must be the baby.' I say. 'Hormones.'

'I don't want to talk about that.'

'Babies make you crave things; you can't help it.'

'Becky…' Rachel warns.

'Tara from work, she craved Pringles dipped in Pesto for months. Guess you won't have to worry about that soon.'

'Rebecca. Stop.'

'Sorry.' I say, rubbing my temples. 'Haven't eaten since breakfast. The wine has gone to my head.' I unwrap my burger, and take a bite. We continue watching *Big Brother* in silence. The argument is still going on, this bald-headed guy yelling at a blonde girl for not telling him she had a kid. They'd kissed in the previous night's episode. I try and concentrate, but the argument makes my head start replaying the conversation I had with Rachel earlier. I think back to the day she arrived at my door at two in the morning, three months ago, bags in hand. I let her in without a word, thinking it would be temporary - I presumed her and Dylan had a fight, and she'd go back in a couple of days. But then a week passed, and another, and another. Every time I had tried to ask her, she changed the topic. Turning my head to Rachel, I press pause on the remote control.

'Hey, I was watching that…' she said.

'What happened between you and Dylan?'

She turns to me. 'What?'

'You've never told me. It's been three months, and you've never told me.'

'I have.'

'You haven't.'

'I have.'

'What then?'

She hesitates. 'He was a dick.'

'How?'

Rachel swallows and doesn't respond.

'How was he a dick?' I repeat.

'Why are you bringing this up?'

'Earlier. You told me to say it's Dylan's.'

'You asked if it was.'

'Thinking you'd say yes.'

'I did.'

'You said most likely.'

'I don't want to talk about it.'

'What happened between you two, Rach?'

Rachel is blushing, and she's picking her nails with her thumb. She always does that when she's trying to think of a lie. She doesn't answer. 'Well?' I persist.

Rachel refuses to look at me when she whispers. 'It's embarrassing.'

'What is?

'It's nothing,' she says, shaking her head.

'Just tell me.'

She swallows, nodding her head slowly. And, after taking a large swig of Pepsi, she does. She tells me about how after being together for ten years, things were starting to get a little routine in certain parts of their life. She says how they were eating spaghetti one night when Dylan first proposed the idea. She wasn't sure at first, but he managed to persuade her into agreeing. She tells me how they spent hours discussing who it would be. Rachel wanted a stranger, Dylan didn't. He knew a guy, apparently, Stephen. They decided to flip a coin in the end. Dylan won. They set a date, invited Stephen over for dinner. Rachel had been nervous all day and drank a lot of wine. So nervous, she forgot to take the pill.

'Most likely Dylan's.' I say, nodding slowly. I get it now. Rachel bites her lip.

'Wait,' I say. 'That still doesn't explain why you left.'

'Doesn't it?'

'There's something you aren't telling me.'

'I'm going to get some more Pepsi. You want anything?' She gets up, starts making her way to the kitchen. I jump up after her, and put my hands on her shoulders, turning her back round.

'You're not getting out of this that easily, Rach.'

'Fine.' Rachel says. 'You want to know what happened?' She shoves my hands off her shoulder and storms to the other side of the room. 'I turned him gay.'

'What?'

'I was out with Sally one night - I got home late, didn't want to wake Dylan up, so I was going to sleep on the sofa, but I heard him upstairs, so I went up and I… I saw him with Stephen!'

I don't know how to react to that. 'Shit Rachel. What did Dylan say?'

'He didn't see me. I came straight to yours.'

'Cheating bastard.'

'That isn't the point, Becky. I turned him gay.'

'I don't think that's how it works, Rach,' I say. 'Why didn't you tell me this before?'

'I dunno,' she mumbles.

'What did you think I would say?'

She shrugs. 'That it was my fault because if I hadn't agreed to his stupid threesome with Stephen, then he wouldn't have seen Stephen's dick and preferred it to mine.'

'You have a dick?'

'I'm being serious Becky.'

'Look,' I say. 'How much did you know about this Stephen guy?'

'Not much. He was a friend of Dylan's from the golf course.'

'That's all?'

Rachel squints, trying to think. 'They went to a golfing convention last summer, spent the weekend there. A couple of other guys were meant to be going, but they couldn't get time off work.'

I shake my head, slowly.

'What?'

'Are you listening to yourself, Rach?'

'What do you mean?'

'Sounds like he spent a lot of alone time with Stephen.'

It takes a while, but finally, her eyes widen. 'I didn't turn him gay?'

'Nope.'

She laughs. 'I knew it!' She puts her hand on her stomach, biting her lip. 'I need to tell him, don't I?'

'I think you should.'

She takes a deep breath, twiddling her thumbs. Eventually, she nods. 'Tomorrow.' There's a long pause.

'Is that why you wanted chicken then? So Dylan wasn't the only one getting cock?'

A Dead End Town

By
Chloe Hodgkinson

It was Christmas Eve. Cody reclined in his dad's tartan armchair, a glass of scotch in his hand, and contemplated moving out of Gold Bridge. He lived alone in what was once his parents' huge log cabin. It was opposite the sign (wooden, with a carving of a miner, and a shelter that kept it from weathering) that welcomed people to the town. Next to it was a flagpole sporting the maple leaf, and a picnic bench. The sign also morbidly displayed the town's decreasing population. Earlier, Cody had parted his drapes once again to see the dwindling number had fallen even further. There were twenty-five people living in Gold Bridge, B.C.

This year there had been a lot of rain which, as well as driving away weekend tourists during the summer, had meant that the earliest snows of the winter hadn't settled. In the past few days the ground had dried out, so Cody knew that the snow that had just started to fall today would last into January.

Cody's Newfoundland, Jessie, barked at the snow.

"What's up, pup?" said Cody. Jessie was the size and colour of a black bear. She loved the snow.

Cody stood up, and the scotch hit him, making his head woozy. His cell had no signal, so he stomped over to the landline – stomping was the only way he could walk straight – and dialled his parents.

"Yeah, Mum… no, it's settling. I know, should have come earlier in the week… no, I don't mind spending Christmas alone… Okay, Mum *okay,* yeah, speak soon, bye."

Cody's parents were just two of the many people who had moved somewhere more accessible than Gold Bridge in the past few years, and Cody was glad of it. The road in and out of town was a long, one-lane, gravel track with a half-hearted white line painted over the top to give the illusion of width. On one side of the road, a ravine led down into Carpenter Lake, on the other; a jagged and insurmountable cliff rose out of the track. Cody's house sat between where the cliff tapered off and where the town of Gold Bridge officially began.

He checked his cupboards - overripe bananas, cans of soup, empty milk carton, empty scotch bottle, no beer. He'd have to go to the grocery store in town before the snow got too thick. Jessie came away from the window when she saw Cody pull on his hiking boots.

"Come on, Jessie, walk." He grabbed a woolly hat and a tennis ball on his way out and was shoved back against the door when Jessie pushed past him to reach the snow. The thermometer outside the door was frozen over. Cody jiggled his heavy iron key into the pine door and used all his strength to lock it.

Valley Hardware and Grocery were having the best business they had gotten all year. People, like the ground squirrels Jessie had chased on their way, were making last-minute preparations for the winter. There were a few other dogs outside the store, and Cody tied Jessie up a few metres away from them.

He was passing the end of the canned food aisle when he saw a flash of bottle-black hair that could only have been his ex-girlfriend, Elise. She was on her own, reaching for a jar from the top shelf. Her new boyfriend, Isaac, the man she had cheated on Cody with was notably absent. Cody was bending down to take a carton of milk from the fridge shelf when she tapped him on the shoulder with a manicured finger.

"Sorry to bother you Cody, but you wouldn't mind getting me a carton of 4%, would you?" Elise said, trying to sweeten her harsh nasal voice. She was heavily pregnant, around eight months, and wearing a loose black dress in lieu of her Chilcotin Hotel blouse.

"Oh, yeah, of course, no problem, Merry Christmas," Cody said, handing her a carton, and starting to push through the other shoppers.

"How are you any-" he heard her say, though he tried to lose her among the hum of Season's Greetings and well wishes the rest of the town were exchanging as they bumped backs in the narrow aisles.

Cody finished collecting his groceries silently, hoping that Elise wouldn't catch him in the queue for the till. He bought plenty of alcohol and a turkey to cook for Christmas dinner that would make sandwiches for the rest of the week.

When Cody and Jessie got home, about four centimetres of snow had settled, some of it on top of the dog making her look less like a Newfoundland than a polar bear. Her eyes had narrowed into happy crescents, and her tongue lolled from between her teeth, catching stray snowflakes and turning them into raindrops. The wind was whipping the storm faster and faster outside the window.

Once he'd put his shopping away, Cody lit the fire with old copies of the *Bridge River Lillooet News* and pulled Jessie's bed closer to it. The television had only picked up static all day, so Cody put on the record player. Chris de

Burgh's *A Spaceman Came Travelling* echoed throughout the house, the crackle of the record layering over the crackle of the fire. With another glass of scotch, Cody settled back into his armchair and let his eyelids droop.

He woke up to Jessie barking loudly at the door. It sounded as if they were beating the wood with their palm. Cody shook off his sleepiness quickly because he had no idea how long the person had been out there. The moment the lock on the door clicked open, Elise burst through.

"Thank god, Cody. What took you so long?" she said. They were the exact same words she had said last year, when she had turned up on Christmas Eve as a surprise, holding a bottle of wine and a sprig of mistletoe.

Elise was shivering; she was wearing the same dress as earlier in the store and a coat that wasn't nearly warm enough. She wore a scarf and hat but no gloves. Her fingers were an icy raw red.

"I was sleeping… why are you here?" Had she not already invited herself inside, had it not been winter, and had she not been pregnant, Cody would have turned Elise away.

Jessie never particularly cared for Elise, so when she had discovered who was at the door, she had padded back to her bed.

"My parents wrote you a card." Elise produced a silver envelope from inside her coat, addressed to 'Janice, Mike & Cody.' It was written in looping handwriting that could easily have been Elise's.

"Oh, thanks," Cody said, ripping through the envelope to reveal a card with a scene of Carpenter Lake in winter. He recognised it as one they sold at the grocery store. "Why don't you sit down. I'm sure I've got some hot cocoa somewhere."

Elise smiled and eased into the chair Cody had been using, nearest the fire. He noticed the glass of scotch on its side – contents on the carpet – next to one of Elise's weather-inappropriate loafer shoes. The snow outside was now at least five inches deep, and the sky was dark.

Cody didn't stir the cocoa when he made it and handed Elise the mug with the spoon left in. He went to sit in the other armchair but stopped before he had lowered into the seat, choosing instead to lean on the mantelpiece. His arm rested in the place where the photo frame containing a picture of him and Elise used to be.

Elise sipped her cocoa and glanced around the room. She had a moist line of chocolatey liquid resting just above her upper lip like the fluffy whipped cream moustaches that Cody used to tell her were cute.

"Cody, do you think you could turn the music off?" said Elise, raising her voice over the record player which was still playing a little too loud for a comfortable conversation.

"Umm sure," replied Cody. He lifted the needle from the record.

"That's better," said Elise, "I've got a headache. Which can't be good for the baby."

"I didn't think that would make any difference to it."

"I'm just trying to look after him, Cody, god." Elise set her mug on the coffee table.

"So, it's a boy?" said Cody, "Congratulations. You two must be very happy."

"You would have known that already if you hadn't ignored me for the past eight months," Elise said. She massaged her baby bump, making eye contact with Cody. He looked away, grumbling and collected the pots he had left around the room the past few days and carrying them through to the kitchen. Elise had no right to be angry at Cody. She had cheated on him, not the other way around. Cody set some glasses on the side and then braced himself against the counter for a moment before re-joining Elise.

"Elise-"

"Cody," said Elise, turning in the chair to face him. "Have you even thought about the possibility that he might be yours?"

"No," Cody lied. He paced over to the window and looked up at the stars that were starting to appear over Gold Bridge. The town shimmered under orange streetlights up the hill, muffled by the greyness of the snow falling almost horizontally.

"I thought it was definitely Isaac's, and as far as I know so does he," said Cody. The grandfather clock chimed six from out in the hallway. Elise stood up and joined Cody, leaning on the windowsill. She angled her body towards Cody but looked into the room rather than at him. Her baby bump was almost touching the top of his thigh.

Elise played with the chain of her necklace, pulling at a chunky silver heart charm and touching it to her lips. Her musky perfume layered headily with the scent of burning. From close up, all the small marks stood out on the dark fabric of Elise's dress. There was a line of foundation smudged into the seam of her low neckline, resting on the swell of her bosom. Elise let go of the charm and swept some hair from her forehead. Her face seemed to be gravitating closer to Cody's than it was before, she closed her eyes and began to part her lips.

"What are you doing, Elise?" said Cody.

Elise withdrew, "I was yawning," she said, covering her mouth and glancing into the night. "It's dark; I should probably get going, right?"

"Um, probably," said Cody. Elise's shoes and coat were by the door, and she waddled off to fetch them. Cody shut the drapes and then met Elise while she was opening the door. The wind shrieked in, and a flurry of snow was blown in and melted onto the carpet. Elise shivered and looked at Cody.

"Well… it was nice seeing you Cody, Merry Christmas," she said.

"Actually, Elise, I don't think you should go out there. I don't think it's safe for a pregnant woman." Cody reached over Elise's head and pushed the door closed. "You should stay here tonight, and I'll take you home in the morning."

"I thought you'd never ask," she said. Elise crossed the room, and manoeuvred herself back onto the sofa, re-minding Cody of a learner driver parking in a bay.

Cody left Elise alone while he thought of where she

might sleep, the guest room perhaps was the obvious choice, though Cody remembered how the mattress wasn't very soft, and of course, it was upstairs. He wasn't entirely sure how pregnant women dealt with stairs. His parents' bedroom then, on the ground floor, sporting the softest mattress and the warmest duvet in the house. Elise poked her head around the door of Cody's parents' bedroom as he was beating some volume into one of the lifeless extra pillows he had found for her. The pillowcase had a garish floral pattern indicative of the pillow's permanent home in the linen cupboard.

"You can sleep here if you like," said Cody, setting the pillow at the head of the bed along with numerous others and drawing up the duvet neatly.

"This is lovely, thank you, Cody," Elise said, drawing the curtains. They met again by the door, "Goodnight," she said. She gave him a gentle but expectant look. For a moment Cody considered how many times he had heard Elise say goodnight, how familiar the words were and the shape of her mouth when she said them.

"Goodnight," said Cody and kissed her on the cheek.

Cody poured himself another glass of scotch and returned to his spot on his chair in the living room. He let Jessie climb up onto his lap, buried his face in her fur, and contemplated not leaving Gold Bridge.

In Other News

By
Daniel Paton

James Mason settled on suicide to end his pain. It would be a minor tragedy in comparison. One life would be over; only a few people would be affected by the loss.

Marcus had no reason to feel any different to normal when he made his breakfast in the shared kitchen the following morning - James rarely was up before 11. Abby had no reason to be worried when she passed his locked door that afternoon on the way back from lunch - he always kept it shut. Ben had no reason to suspect anything unusual when James wasn't present at their 4:15 History lecture - he often didn't show up. Leanne was totally indifferent to his absence in the kitchen that evening - she didn't know or like him that much anyway.

The whole of the flat and many of the block got a good night's rest, and it wasn't until the day after that anyone suspected anything. It was very out of character for James to be offline from Facebook for a few hours, let alone an entire day. A couple of coursemates who he had socialised with a bit, noticed this and messaged him.

> Hey there, what you up to? Just
> checking you're okay :)

A few hours after, with no reply, they got a little bit worried. One of them messaged Ben, who replied that he had probably just gone home for a day or two.

James had friends back home, but since they all went separate ways to start university in their various locations a couple of weeks ago, they had been too busy adjusting to their new lives to talk much. His parents hadn't contacted him for a few days either, having decided not to be too clingy with their son, and let him enjoy his new independence.

While a state of mild concern spread, James sat in the en-suite bathroom of his small, characterless room. The tiles were on the yellow side, having seen years of use without consistent cleaning. The room had been a temporary home to 21 students; now it was a temporary coffin for James Mason. The blood had stopped dribbling out of his ruined wrist, but it was the overdose that had killed him anyway, the slashing was just a failsafe. He was wearing a shirt with the sleeves rolled up, some loose fitting jeans, and a peaceful expression. He had been dead for almost 72 hours before he was found. The security guard, a small balding man with retirement in his sights, called in by Ben to open the door to James's room, cried on the spot when he saw the body. An ambulance and a police car turned up on campus, as the security guard herded James's flatmates into the kitchen and made sure they didn't see what he had.

The block group-chat was buzzing with questions about all the drama.

> What's going on?? Police and
> ambulance??
> Someone hit the sesh too hard or
> something?!
> Hope everyone is alright x

Ben, Abby, Marcus and Leanne saw their phones lighting up with messages but didn't reply.

'Should we say it's our flat?' Abby asked

'No.' Marcus replied, 'people have probably already seen them come up here.'

'Can you just tell us what's going on?' Ben asked the security guard, who was stood by the door, with watery eyes.

He shook his head.

'I think we all know what's happened.' Leanne said, staring at the floor.

Ben stood up and paced around. 'Fucking hell.'

They had already assumed the worst and were proven correct when they saw two medics carrying the body bag along the corridor and down the stairs.

Small groups, gathered by windows and doors, saw the bag as it was carried out to the ambulance. A couple of pictures were taken. Before the night was over, social media had carried the message to most of the university: a student was dead.

It was hours before any of them mustered the courage to go back to their rooms, as it would mean having to pass James's. They looked up at the security guard, expecting some answer, some instruction, some consolation, but got nothing apart from a whisper before he departed, "I'm sorry".

'You know,' Abby said to them, afterwards, 'they're going to blame us.'

'But we didn't know...' Marcus trailed off, unable to explain the feeling of confusion.

'He seemed alright,' Ben added, 'like, he never showed any sign that he was, so... so unhappy.'

'I guess it doesn't always show.' Leanne said, expressionless, before leaving the room. She would drop out of university a couple of weeks later.

'But you have to be seriously... Low for you to even consider...' Ben couldn't bring himself to say it, 'Fucking hell.'

There was silence before an outburst from Marcus,'Hang on a second, hang on! We don't even know what happened, I know what you're doing, you're all assuming that he... Killed himself! But we don't know that! It could have been anything, a heart attack, an illness, or just some freak accident!

Abby shook her head, 'If that was the case, they would have just said it, surely? But no, they wouldn't say, because it's worse than that because it's more...sensitive.'

'Jesus,' Ben said, 'his parents don't even know yet do they.'

Anna and Robert Mason were in bed sleeping soundly. She was shivering from the cold that was being allowed to get to her body because Robert was, as usual, hogging the duvet. They had been married for 23 years and had lived in this house for almost 20. It seemed so quiet now that their child had left them like they had less purpose. They were still getting used to his absence from their home.

The news would come to them in the morning, just before they left for work. A young police woman would tremble as she tried to explain that their only son, who they had loved more than anything, who they done everything they could for, who they thought was away enjoying himself, had taken his own life.

The identity of the deceased spread quickly and by morning, people who had never known or met James were now talking about him. Tributes were made on Twitter and Facebook.

R.I.P James :(

Unsure exactly how to act, everyone left the block looking as serious as they felt they should.

Behind the scenes in the university, conversations

were being held, and meetings were being arranged. James's designated personal tutor, Dr Jane Horton, was one of the one's being called on, but she hadn't even met him. He was just a name on her list of students, and she was working through them alphabetically to organise meetings with them.

A minute of silence was held before the History lecture commenced that afternoon. Bob Kale, leaned over his lectern, staring at the white space between his notes. A shadow hung over the corner of the spacious room that James used to occupy, and no one, not even those couple of students who would have usually sat with him, dared go there. The silence was broken before the time was up when Ben opened the door and sat down awkwardly.

He felt eyes on him throughout the hour-long seminar. A coursemate popped up on messenger to him halfway through.

```
Are you okay? Here to talk if you
            want :)
```

He stared at the message and felt annoyed. It wasn't the first like it, and it wouldn't be the last.

Everyone is "here" for me, he thought, *maybe if they had been "there" for him, then he wouldn't be dead.*

He replied:

```
I' m fine, but thanks.
```

Then, after a moment's consideration added a :) to assert his fineness and seem more polite. Maybe they were, but maybe he pushed them away like I'm doing now.

Anna and Robert were sitting on a bench near the town centre. They had walked aimlessly away from the hospital, where they had just been to the mortuary. When they had been informed of the news that morning, Anna had flown into hysterics of disbelief, while Robert was overcome by numbness. On the drive over, they hadn't been able to talk. He saw the body, but she refused to.

She shook her head, claiming it was all a dream. Now, sat together, because they didn't know what to do or where to go, they still didn't know how to talk. So they didn't. He was desperate to be close, but she wanted to get a million miles away. He tried to put his arm around her, but she flinched. He touched her hand, but she pulled hers away. She was staring at the ground, still shaking her head, while his eyes were fixed on her, pleading.

'Anna,' he managed.

And at last she fell into him. She buried her head into his coat and sobbed, while he allowed tears to drip out of his weary eyes. People walked past; some noticed them, some didn't, but none of them could share their pain. Some looked at them for longer than they normally would. A photography student subtly took a picture of them.

Ben, Marcus and Abby gathered in the kitchen that evening, Leanne was nowhere to be found.

'How was everyone's day then?' Abby asked them.

There was no response. 'Well then...'

'I'm going out.' Marcus stated, going to the fridge and opening a bottle of vodka.

'Seriously?' Ben said to him.

'Yep. You wanna come? Few people off my course, no one in this block, so shouldn't have to deal with all the... Shit.'

Ben shook his head.

Abby reflected out loud, 'Maybe if we'd invited him out more...'

'Fuck sake.' Marcus took a big swig from the bottle and left.

After a few seconds of silence, Abby asked Ben, 'Is everyone showing you loads of sympathy?'

'Yep.'

'Is it making you feel guilty?'

'Yep.'

The Student Support Zone were gathered, along with a few heads of departments and the director, to discuss what had happened, and what could be done to improve student wellbeing. It was agreed that things would have to change. Talks were to be booked on depression, mental health, and suicide awareness. Emails would be sent more frequently, inviting students to take advantage of the free counselling and support sessions available.

The funeral was held a couple of weeks later. Robert and Anna put in a note in a newspaper, an open invitation for anyone who knew him to come along. Some friends from his school-days came, Ben and Abby were there, Marcus and Leanne weren't. A couple of coursemates were, his Personal Tutor wasn't, nor were any of the university staff. The church that the Mason family had frequented years earlier wasn't as full or lively as it had been on those Sundays. It was a patchwork of black clothing, bowed heads and bleary eyes.

It was a scene that James had pictured as he bled out on his bathroom floor, with waves of warmth pushing him further and further away from his body. Something he saw on the news just a few weeks before flashed into his mind. A mass vigil that took place for those who were killed in a terror attack, and hundreds of people rallied around; they stood in silence for a while before spontaneously breaking into a song of defiance. It was powerful, cinematic even, and made anyone watching, let alone attending, well up with emotional. The thought of his parents made him wish he had written something. He knew they would never recover, and wanted to be able to explain that they were amazing, that there was nothing else they could have done, that he was doing this for himself. He felt a stab of anger in his chest for not even being able to die right. The thoughts of others' reactions did not distress him, for he knew that their upset would be temporary. His highschool friends would be upset, but they would get over it, as would his flatmates. The flutter of caring around university would fade, and maybe things would even change for the better.

His head slumped back against the dirty tiles, and he let out a gentle breath, which would be his last.

It was less than a month before a new student moved in.

Inside

By
Cieran Cooper

Becky pulled up outside the school. She could see that the top car park was still packed with cars. Kids were getting in as soon as their parents pulled up to collect them after the long school day. She was careful to avoid eye contact with Hector; the on-duty teacher. He stood there, checking his watch frequently as he waited for the parents to collect their kids. She could see Morgan standing on the pavement with the other kids, waiting for his ride. From there, she could see the sweat drizzling down his face, the shaving rash which coated his jaw. Becky thought to turn around and go back, but she saw the slender, slightly toned body shape masked by the school shirt. She carried on into the waiting area and stayed there for a moment until he came towards the car.

'Hi.' Morgan said as he got in.

'Hey.'

He looked at the dashboard then shifted and took a look at the seat under him. No longer was there a flock of crumbs hiding in the ridges. 'Cleaned your car?'

'It needed it.'

He waited for a moment. He looked over at Becky, then at the school car park. 'I like your hair. It's a nice change.'

'Thanks. I'm not so sure on it myself. I think it makes me look old.'

'Nothing could make you look old.'

She moved her hand through her hair and gazed at the sky. The hue of colour from the white clouds matched the school buildings as they baked in the sun. 'I don't think this should happen tonight. I need to think about it some more.'

Morgan moved his hand over to her neck. He gently gave it a stroke before tilting her head towards him. 'Why?'

'It's not right.'

'It's perfectly fine.'

She turned her head towards the road. 'I wish it was.'

'If you really want to do it another night we'll wait.'

'Yeah. We'll do it another night. You got your key?'

'I think so.' He reached into his left trouser pocket and felt around for the key. His fingers touched the ridged point. 'Yep.'

She started the car and began the journey to Morgan's home. 'Your mum okay?'

'Yeah, she's alright.'

Becky checked the rear-view mirror and watched as Hector and the remaining school kids drifted out of sight. She thought about the way in which Morgan used to be one of those stranded there. How she used to offer him lifts, and he'd be hesitant as if still thinking of those childish talks with his mum where he'd be told about strangers. 'You should be with her, supporting her.'

'I can't. She just wells up, and all I can do is sit there, say it'll be okay when I don't know it will.'

She dropped him off at his home and then returned

to her house.

A week later, Becky brought a bottle and two wine glasses into the living room. She placed them on the coffee table, then sat down as she waited for him to arrive. The doorbell rang, she opened it and let him in.

As he patted his boots dry on the hessian doormat, he looked at the empty picture frames plastering the right wall. 'Why haven't you used these?'

She gave herself a moment to take a breath. It brought back the memories of the photos that used to sit within the square frames. The photos of her and Kevin on their wedding day, and the ones of Kevin's nieces and nephews who she'd only met once or twice. She didn't reply to Morgan. Instead, she went into the living room and leaned back into the blue leather settee.

He followed her in. He sat down and turned to face her.

She offered him a glass of wine.

'I shouldn't.'

She watched as his face, trapped in the brightness which plumed from the lamp beside him, contorted as he avoided looking at the glass. 'It's fine. It's one drink.'

'You know I shouldn't.'

'Okay. I'll need it though.' She poured herself a glass, took a sip of it and then placed it on the table. Her eyes remained on the glass while they sat in silence for a moment. She picked it up and took another sip.

'How's the studying going?'

He swept himself into the corner of the settee. 'Alright.'

'Meaning?'

'Well, it's a little tough to concentrate.'

She stayed silent for a moment, contemplating her answer. 'I can ask Hector to get your tutors to give you a little more help if you want.'

He moved to look at her. 'No. I don't really want anyone else knowing about it.'

'I could help. I could try to learn the syllabus.'

'Thanks, but it would be a lot of trouble for you.'

She looked right at him, refusing to blink or divert her attention. 'I don't mind.'

'Maybe.'

She sat up straight and swivelled herself to face Morgan. His cheeks were buried beneath acne. As was his forehead. It told the truth the rest of him never seemed to. 'Funny what a difference ten years does to you.'

'It's not that much.'

'Enough to leave my days of having spots far behind me.'

He reached his left hand up and felt his face. 'Some adults still get them.'

'Unlucky ones, yeah.'

He got up and wandered around the room, looking at the pictures hanging on the walls. He pointed to one. 'This painting's really nice.'

'Yeah. I like it. I never envisioned it staying there though.'

'Really?'

'Things just didn't turn out how I expected.' She leaned forwards and poured herself another glass of wine.

He took his phone from his pocket, checked the time and then put it back. 'It's getting on.'

'We have plenty of time. Got your grades for that art piece?'

'No. We were meant to get it weeks ago, but it's taking longer to mark than my teacher expected.'

Becky went to the window. She looked at the houses facing hers, tried to peer through the slithers of gaps between their curtains. She could see nothing but the lights in the living rooms but wondered about what was happening there. She thought about how any one of those houses could have someone with the same dilemma she had, and the ones that could have something worse.

Morgan walked up behind her and placed his arms around her waist. 'I missed you yesterday.'

She leant into his grip and moved her head, so her face brushed against his neck. 'How did it go?'

'She's been kept in.'

She thought about the trips to the hospital she'd made two years ago. The way she'd felt she never wanted to be there. The fake smiles to soothe Kevin. Bringing Kevin's clean clothes and taking back his dirty ones was a hassle she didn't need on top of everything but there had been no one else to help. No one else to rely on. She released herself from his grip, turned, and gave him a hug.

'I wish I hadn't mentioned it to Ricky.'

She stayed silent and just kept her eyes concentrated on his face. She watched his eyes rise to look at her, then tilt down to the floor.

'He told all the rest of the guys.'

'So? They care. I've seen how they've taken an interest in what's happening.'

'Exactly. It's changed things.' He brushed his blonde hair out of the way of his eyes.

She moved and kissed him. He reciprocated, moving his tongue into her mouth. It wasn't like the other times; something felt different. She brought herself out of the kiss and went to sit back on the settee. She thought of his mum. The cold, empty place she was in. The way she would be feeling alone and distraught given what happened yesterday. 'Go upstairs. I'll be up in a moment.'

Morgan looked at her, saw how her body was angled away from him so he couldn't see her face. He went upstairs.

She got up from the settee and locked the front door and went upstairs. She thought of Hector's face if he found out about it. The news would slither into his office off the tongue of some little kid who thought it was their duty to report it. Morgan would receive counselling; she'd never be allowed near a school again. He'd probably learn to forget about her while her life would be a wreck. She thought about the way people would try to find her guilty of grooming tons of other children, just because she was nice to them. All of the hockey group would be looked at with suspicion. The trips to the cinema would be seen as a way for her to get close to them. Her friends would desert her; her family would neglect her. She'd have no one.

He was sitting on the edge of the double bed. Becky looked at him, looked at the bloodshot eyes which stared back at her. The yawn that he tried to conceal behind his hand.

He pulled at his shirt, making the crisp cotton sweep across his body. He grabbed hold of the button at the top of his jeans and undid them. The jeans clung to his legs as he brought them down to his ankles. He slid them over the heels of his feet and slung them onto the floor. 'I'm ready.'

'You think we're doing it while I'm in this dress and you're still in those Mickey Mouse boxers?'

'I guess not.'

She dragged her crimson silk dress slowly off of her top half and brought it down to the floor. The dress swirled into a small circle on the floor of the bedroom as she brought her knickers down to her knees. She released her bra and let that drop to the ground, revealing her goose-bumped body. Looking over at Morgan, she saw his shaped stomach. The small scrolls of muscle on his belly peeked out from behind his arms. She brought her gaze down, saw the little clump of pubic hair below his navel and the six inches of penis which pointed towards her.

She reached over to the vanity and slid open the top drawer. She moved the letters and bills from inside, only to reveal a photo of her and Kevin. The picture showed him standing beside her holding a glass of wine in his hand as they were photographed at their wedding reception. She thought how they'd seen themselves being together for the rest of their futures. She moved it onto the top of the vanity, allowing her to see the condoms she'd kept below it. She reached for one and held it for a few moments. Her eyes then flicked back to the photo. She set the condom back, piled the bills and letters on top, and pushed the draw into its socket.

'We can't do this.'

'Are you okay?'

Becky stood there for a second in silence. 'I don't know. I think it's best we go downstairs, actually.'

'Why?'

'We shouldn't be doing this.'

'I thought this is what we both wanted.'

'We did. I, I still do. But we can't.'

He waited there for a moment, watching as Becky's hair rippled in the wind that came through the open window. He looked at her. They both stayed in that position for a moment, neither one able to look away. He then picked his clothes and pulled on his jeans. He made his way downstairs.

She waited for a moment. She looked at the photo on top of her vanity. She thought about the choice she'd just made; the choices she'd made for him all those times. The way she'd resisted all temptation to stay loyal and devoted. She would stay so for the time being. She put the photo back and went downstairs.

Becky and Morgan got into her car. She placed her keys in the ignition and struck her headlights on. Now able to see clearly, she drove him to his house. She watched as he went in, looking at the front room's curtains, the light that seeped through the gap, and wondered what was going on inside.

The Bathroom

By
Isabella Blackburn

Marianne stood in the bathroom reflected on all sides by mirrors. She was staring at the fish vase in her hand. The fat fish was mossy green and curved into the palm of her hand, its mouth gaping. She stood in front of an oval mirror, if she looked up, she would see herself from all angles.

She remembered the beach in Montauk, the little hotel with fish vases on all the tables. The year she was twenty-three and her sister Alexis had been transferred to New York by her company. Marianne, employed and free, had been able to go and visit her as a birthday present. She remembered scouring Manhattan for birthday cake ingredients.

They walked along the rise of the beach in the cold

April evening. The savage waves crashed onto the sand, sending spray up into the air. Their feet sank with each step as they faced into the wind. Marianne raised her face to the sky, filled her lungs and tasted salt.

As they walked abreast in silence. Marianne glanced sideways at Alexis. She cleared her throat.

'There is something that I've been wanting to ask you,' she said. 'About what happened to Papa.'

Alexis watched the waves, seemed oblivious. Marianne's hands were fists in her pockets. She licked her lips, felt the sting of the sea spray on her face.

'Why did you tell her? You promised me you wouldn't tell her.'

'What are you talking about?' Alexis asked, turning guiltless eyes to look at Marianne.

Marianne paused, she could let it go, brush it off, keep walking. Ignore the questions that had been lodged in her throat for so long. They were in a strange land, and she would be leaving in few days. But she had to know. She needed peace from the guilt, or if not peace then a chance to share it.

'The thing I told you about Papa, the reason I left home.'

'What thing? I have no idea what you are talking about. He was ill Marianne; you know that. Who do you mean by her?' asked Alexis.

Marianne thought she could hear an edge to her voice, a slight tremor. Maybe it wasn't there at all only she thought it should be. 'Mamma. *That* her. You told her, even after you swore not to.' Marianne sucked in a breath with the effort of keeping her voice even. She felt the pain in her throat, digging into her.

'Swore not to tell Mamma what? You're sounding really dramatic Marianne.' Alexis laughed, shaking her head, her eyes sweeping over the waves, the beach. She wiped her face with her sleeve.

Marianne didn't believe her; it was impossible to forget. She remembered each word, every moment. They had played over and over.

'We were at Mamma's, in the bathroom. You were giving me a hard time about leaving home,' said Marianne.

'Hang on, that was what? Eight years ago? I remember that you were too young to be leaving home. You weren't even sixteen, were you? She was worried about you,' said Alexis.

'She wasn't worried about me! She was worried about other people finding out everything that was going on.' Marianne felt her voice rising. She took a deep breath, clenched her teeth, then continued more quietly. 'Anyway, that's not the point. The point is that you were yelling at me, remember? You were telling me how I was being selfish and thoughtless.'

'I don't remember that.' Alexis increased her pace and Marianne hurried to keep up with her.

'And I told you why and then made you promise not to tell. And you swore.'

They stopped walking, Marianne looked back at the waves. It was wild and desolate here, the day darkening steadily. She swallowed the salt trickling down her throat. She had said it so quietly that she didn't know if Alexis heard her. She felt as though her head would drag off her neck with the weight of it but that it was full of cotton at the same time.

'And then you told her, I should have known you would. You've always been a mammas' girl.'

They stood facing the wild waves, but Marianne's mind was elsewhere.

Alexis stood over her as she sat on the divan in the bathroom.

'What are you doing? You have to stop messing around and come home,' said Alexis

Marianne hunched into herself. She had come to see Alexis, who was back from school for the Christmas holidays. She shouldn't have come.

'You don't know what she's like. I can't live here. I'm not coming back.'

'I can't believe you're being so bloody selfish. Do you ever think of anyone but yourself? You don't go to school, and now you've taken off. You should be at home not... wherever you are. Where are you living? How could you do this to her?' Alexis paused, waiting for an answer but Marianne said nothing, which question would she answer anyway? Alexis clenched her fists, raising them towards her and Marianne thought, she wants to slap me again.

'She's really upset. She said she's at her wit's end and has no idea why you're doing this to her. What is your problem? Are you going to answer me?' Alexis shouted. She sounds like an irate mother, not an older sister, thought Marianne. Not like their mother though.

Alexis stood by the vanity, between her and the door.

'You don't understand. You've been away at school since we moved back to London. You're hardly ever here. You have no idea what it's like. She kicked him out and then kept calling him at Granny's demanding that he come back. She's drunk all the time, and she's vicious.' Marianne squeezed the words out.

'That's not true! She's not drunk now, and she hasn't been the whole time I've been back. I would know if she was drinking. You're lying; you always were such a liar...'

Marianne wanted to leave, she eyed the door and pictured shoving Alexis out of the way and running out of the bathroom, along the hallway, out of the front door and away, never coming back. Or curling up until she consumed herself and left an empty space for Alexis to rant at. Alexis kept on, and the noise became unbearable.

Marianne recognised her own voice speaking, interrupting, but she had no control over the words. Didn't even know where they came from.

'I left because Papa tried to rape me.'

Her sister gaped at her. The tirade had stopped abruptly, and Marianne breathed into the momentary silence.

Then Alexis opened her mouth, and Marianne saw the questions coming. She said rapidly, 'Don't tell anyone! Promise me you won't tell anyone. Especially not her. It's fine, nothing bad happened. But I can't be here anymore, ok?'

Alexis was still staring at her, 'He wouldn't do that. You're lying,' she said.

Marianne stood up, intent on getting out. She could feel her hands shaking. She stood up close to Alexis. 'You have to swear that you won't tell. He's sick. He didn't mean to; it will make everything worse. Swear it!'

'I… I won't say anything, I swear.' Alexis said, her hands had fallen to her sides, and she had stepped back. Marianne was so glad she had finally stopped yelling, she headed for the door.

'I have to go, welcome home Sis.' As she grabbed the door handle, the little brass locking hook swung, tapping on the wood and she glanced at it.

She recalled the moment of lying in the bath; there was a knock on the door, her father walked in and went into the separate loo behind the old door at the other end of the bathroom. Towels hung off the back of it, and old glass panels were painted over in yellowing white paint. He glanced at her and smiled on the way out, then pulled the door shut behind him.

'There needs to be a lock on the bathroom door.' Her mother had said to her father. 'It's not right for you to be able to wander in when the girls are in the bath. They are too old for that now.'

And the little brass hook and eye was added to the door.

'I don't remember any of that. Why do we have to talk about it? It was a long time ago, what difference would it make?' said Alexis. 'I told you, he was ill, really ill. You know he was.'

Marianne was starting to believe it, that she really didn't remember. She almost envied her the ignorance.

'It was my fault.' she said. 'I should never have told you, and then none of it would have happened. I told the Social Worker what would happen if they kept on. I begged her just to leave it, but she wouldn't.'

Alexis said nothing, she stood frowning, staring out to

sea. Marianne watched her and imagined that she wanted to block her ears, shut her words out. There would be no sharing this; it was hers to carry alone. She deserved it. Marianne took Alexis by the hand and began to pull her back the way they had come.

'I'm sorry, you're right. It won't make any difference. Let's not talk about this anymore, like you said it was a long time ago.' She hugged herself. 'It's freezing! Come on, let's head back, we can sit by the fire and warm up. I'm hungry.' She turned and started to stomp back along her footprints. It was almost dark. Further down the beach, she could see the warm lights of the hotel waving in the misty air. She pulled Alexis along with her. She felt like they were just outlines in the dusky air.

The hotel was warm and bright after the chilled darkness outside; a fire burned in the living room. They had a glass of wine sitting in cosy armchairs and then had dinner in the quaint dining room and, on the table was the fish vase.

'Look at this. It's so cute. Mamma would love it,' said Alexis

'It is really pretty. She would like it, she could add it to her collection,' Marianne said.

'Do you think they would let us buy one?' asked Alexis.

'There are lots of them,' said Marianne waving an arm around the other tables. 'They probably wouldn't miss one.'

Marianne thought back to when she sat at the top of the stairs out of sight. There were men banging on the bathroom door and the little brass hook held fast. The door was locked, and her father was in there. The narrow hallway was full of bodies, they were shouting. 'David! Can you hear me, can you open the door? Open the door, David. Can you let us know if you're alright?'

Marianne gently put the vase back on the vanity and glanced at her reflections. The story played out again in her mind.

She released the brass hook, walked to her mother's room. Behind the closed door, she could hear the muffled sound of the TV. She opened the door and looked in, the smell of stale cigarettes and alcohol hit her, and she coughed. A figure was huddled under the cover.

'I'm going now Mamma,' she said loudly. The shape didn't move, but she knew she had been heard. She shut the bedroom door, let herself out and headed home.

Summer in Southampton

By
Mark Webber

As an English teacher in a summer language school, I looked on the group leaders who accompanied the students from their home countries with disdain. During lessons, while we laboured to din a few nuggets of language into the unwilling heads of their young charges, they eschewed all responsibility for them and swanned off for coffee in the nearest town. Later, when the students were enjoying a visit to nearby cultural centres (aka McDonald's and the Disney Store), or a workout on the sports field, the leaders could sit back and relax, safe in the knowledge that our staff would handle any crisis. So when an Italian friend offered to pay me to accompany her with a group to a language school in Southampton, I almost had to be physically restrained from biting her hand off.

I met the group at Heathrow and travelled down with them in the coach. Before we even hit the outskirts of Southampton, I suspected that my dream of an idyllic stay in restful circumstances was pure moonshine. No more than three hours out of the *Bel Paese* one member of the group was already desperately homesick. This was no tot, tearful at being prematurely wrenched from hearth and home, but an 18-year-old school leaver due to depart that autumn for a university city hundreds of miles from her home in Abruzzo.

By the time we reached the University of Southampton, which was to be our base for the next couple of weeks, the girl (I'll call her Cinzia) was close to hysteria. I know enough about the irrational nature of fear not to pooh-pooh others' terrors, and I felt sympathy for her; not so her fellow students though. Most of them subscribed to the 'pull yourself together' school of psychological counselling.

By next morning Cinzia was declaring that she absolutely could not remain any longer. She even hinted at suicide if she were prevented from departing. This left me, and my colleague Fiorella, with a three-pronged problem: there was no one to accompany the girl on her return journey. Her ticket could not easily be altered, and just to show that nothing is ever easy, she was part of a small sub-group who were due to stay on for a third week after the main party had returned home at the end of the second. One of the group leaders had rashly consented to remain with that group after their colleague had departed. I don't intend to dwell on the identity of this foolish person, beyond saying that it was not Fiorella.

I had a plan for the first day of the school; once the students were safely in their lessons, I would catch a bus into the city centre. There I would take in the pre-Raphaelites in the Municipal Art Gallery and then linger over several cappuccinos in the *Piccolo Mondo* café nearby. Fiorella would naturally be welcome to accompany me if this plan met with her approval. (Yes, I did already know my way around Southampton.) Instead, we spent nearly two hours in a phone box, calling everybody imaginable; parents, agents, airlines and on and on. The outcome? Stasis!

That was the pattern for very nearly two weeks. Hours of futile telephoning. Nothing changed, except that our frustration mounted. Meanwhile, Cinzia whined and threatened all manner of imprecisely-defined self-harm while continuing to take part in lessons and activities; and her fellow students' antipathy for her grew steadily. If they had been familiar with the term 'drama queen' I am sure her companions would have said that it summed up their attitude perfectly.

It would have been nice to be able to report that one instance of teenage angst apart, our stay in Southampton was a walk in the park. But alas, as it went on it took on the character of another kind of walk altogether: Frodo's anguished tramp into the land of Mordor. The main cause of the problem was one of the other groups in the school. Among the various nationalities present, there was a group of Druses from Israel. I knew the name from news reports of various episodes of unpleasantness in the Middle East, particularly in Lebanon. There was a time when you could scarcely open a newspaper without reading about the doings of the Druse militia. But who exactly were they?

There were some thirty boys in the Druse party, ranging in ages from 14 to 19. They were accompanied by a Druse adult who spoke little English and one of their teachers, a young Jewish man who had more or less fluent English. We cultivated his acquaintance assiduously, and he was the source of all our information about them.

It seemed that the Druses were an exclusive ethnic group present in many of the countries of the Middle East, whose ties to other Druses elsewhere in the region were more important than their links to other ethnic or religious groups in their own countries. They had their own religion, similar to but distinct from Islam, and their own form of social organisation. There was no scope at all for outsiders to join the Druse community. Either you were born a Druse or you weren't, and no Druse could leave without earning the obloquy of others. Anyone who did leave was as though dead to the others. Naturally, marrying outside the community was unthinkable. Opportunities for Druse women were strictly limited. They received little education, were not free to travel (hence the absence of females amongst the party) and had scant freedom over the choice of marriage partners.

It didn't take us long to work out that we were faced with a situation of explosive potential. We were sharing accommodation with a group of young men from a background which, to us, seemed positively medieval, who for the first time in their lives found themselves in a modern western environment. They were all extremely fit and obviously spent a large part of their free time engaging in some form of sport. Their hormones were already on overdrive. Now, instead of the repressed, submissive, and shrouded girls of their own community, they saw young western girls in the process of learning what it meant to be a woman; and, what's more, we were in the middle of a hot summer when nobody cared too much to cover up. You could see from the look on the faces of the Druse boys that they didn't know where they had ended up or how they were supposed to behave. A lot of them adopted a rather aggressive demeanour, though if you looked into their eyes, you could see the insecurity inside.

The organisation of the school could be summed up in one word: lacking. One area where it lacked impinged on us right from the start; allocation of rooms. We struggled to discern any pattern in the way rooms were allocated to the different groups. Our students found themselves living cheek by jowl with those of other nationalities. Ordinarily, I would have said that was no bad thing; in the interests of cultural and linguistic exchange, unfettered mixing is desirable. But several of our girls found themselves sharing a corridor with some of the Druse boys. They found that highly intimidating. They reported that, whenever they left their rooms to go to the bathroom, they had to run the gauntlet of little knots of Druses who appeared to follow them with their eyes. Of course, how much of this was genuine intimidation and how much the creation of the girls' own imaginations, stoked up by the doom merchants among their friends, it was impossible to say. In any event, the fact that they perceived a problem was enough to mean that there was one.

One or two of the more impulsive characters among the Italian boys were all for going and sorting things out with the Druse boys in a rather Neanderthal fashion. One of them, though only sixteen, would have scared me if I'd come upon him in a dark alley. Lorenzo, as I'll call him, played rugby for the Italian under-18 national side. He was built like a tank and had no neck – his head grew directly out of his shoulders. These boys were firmly reminded that others were responsible for the well-being of the girls and that an intervention of the kind they proposed would have been disastrous. We managed to get the girls moved to new rooms where they felt more at ease and began a rather more long-winded, painstaking process for resolving the problem with the Druses: we made friends with them.

Some of the Druses proved quite amenable. We made a lot of progress in winning their trust during the two weeks. Others though never did quite overcome their suspicions of us. Eventually, we managed to establish an uneasy sort of truce which enabled us all to rub along together. There were still odd flashpoints, like the disco, when cultural differences caused tension. The Druse boys thought that if they wanted to dance with certain girls, that was their right; the Italian boys vowed that no Druse boys would "steal" their girls and the girls didn't always seem to know what they wanted.

Add to all of that a catalogue of other niggles about the school – dull, uninspiring lessons, activities that failed to engage the students, lacklustre excursions, including one trip to Bournemouth which got off to a disastrous start when the bus broke down half way, and late-night noise from students and teachers, which kept everyone else awake – and it becomes clear that the overall experience fell woefully short of expectations.

At last, the time arrived for Fiorella to depart with the bulk of the students, leaving me with the remainder. Cinzia, the girl with the desperate longing for home, went with her. She had managed to persuade one of the others, a boy who had discovered a yearning for further experience of England, to swap tickets with her. I found out later though that all had not gone smoothly at the airport. An *Al Italia* official had declared "La ragazza non parte" (the girl is not travelling). Apparently, the ticket swap was not permitted and would not be honoured. Only after lengthy pleading and cajoling could Fiorella persuade that stern bureaucrat to relent.

The rest of us settled down to enjoy our final week, but our hearts weren't really in it. The others were missing their companions and had belatedly realised that two weeks of summertime lessons, when their schoolmates back in Italy were at the beach, were more than enough. For my part, I was rueing my harsh thoughts about the group leaders. I realised now that they more than earned their money. My own life had been on hold since I had arrived in Southampton and I wanted it back.

When I finally waved goodbye to those few remaining students at Heathrow and set off for home, a free man with responsibility only for myself for the first time in three weeks, there was one thing I had resolved: to stick to what I knew. I was a teacher of English as a foreign language. At the end of my lessons, I handed over responsibility for my students to someone else. That was how it had been before and how it would be again. To interfere with the natural order of things could only lead to sorrow. A valuable lesson had been learnt.

Inner Secrets

By
Courtney Hulbert

He caught her eye across the open plan corridor. He sat awkwardly in a suit. On this occasion he was glad not to be in uniform, true, but this was just another form of uniform, which he hated it. Give him the woods and plains of the free land and his radio equipment any day. Moving his hand, she saw the movement. A flick of the wrist up and down, a gesture that could be badly misinterpreted but here meant 'Want a brew?', then spreading his fingers: 'Five minutes?' He saw a flicker of a frown and an only-just shake of the head. Then her eyes left him and returned to the speaker of her impromptu meeting across the corridor.

It was strange being public in this secret world where you unexpectedly bumped into people you expected to bump into. He turned to his own briefing, but ignored the man holding court. It couldn't hold his attention. He hated the way they carried on, like fugitives escaping the relationship police. He wanted to open the roof of the cage and let the bird fly free. And in just one week he'd be five thousand miles away, and it would just, could only, get worse. If something happened to him, how would she know? Minutes later he saw her meeting break up. He saw her flash him a glance beneath her eyebrows then she walked away with her colleagues. Watching her walk away broke his heart. He even forgot to admire the sway of her bum.

'It's not a twitch.

'Huh?'

'It's not a twitch. Who was he with?' The man flicked a page on the clipboard he held loosely at his side.

'Signals Corps.'

'It's a code. Morse maybe. Yeah, Morse code. It's not a twitch; he's telling us something. It's Morse code, look at the rhythm.'

The doctor watched the man's eyelids. Sure enough, there was a pattern. He felt a glimmer of excitement. Maybe there was hope. He had never known a triple amputee with these head injuries to have survived so long. What a will the man must have. 'Get someone who speaks Morse code. Get them now.'

The soldier was uncomfortable. He didn't like hospitals. There were enough references to dying in his day job without having it thrust in his face. He took off his beret and crushed it in his hand, stuffing it into a pocket of his combat trousers. They waited. Machines hummed, interpreting life. Drips dripped, giving it.

'He's on,' said the nurse. The machines said nothing, but the tension in the room built. Nothing could measure that. The soldier looked down at the man in the bed, eyes shut above the oxygen mask, drip-lines caging him in. His eyelid flickered, more a movement of the eyebrow and the socket than the lid itself. This wasn't communicating; this was a freak show.

'What's he saying?'

'How the fuck should I know?' he thought it was nothing, but then he saw something he recognised. His brain didn't pick it up, his soul did. 'G, G for Golf,' the soldier whispered. Something had got hold of him now; something gripped him. Awe? 'Golf Echo Tango Mike Echo.'

The doctor and nurse looked at each other. They were trying to decipher the cypher inside the crypt inside the code in their heads. At what point did it become English?

'Get me?' said the doctor having distilled the phonetics. 'What does that mean?'

'No, there's a space,' said the soldier. 'Get me. 'Get me' … something.'

'He's stopped,' said the nurse. 'The poor dear must be exhausted.'

'Mike Alpha Yankee.' The soldier started again. 'Zulu Tango.'

'Mayzt? Is that English?'

'Does he speak any other languages?' asked the nurse.

'Is his wife still in the building? Get his wife.'

'She went home,' said the nurse. 'To look after the kids.'

'His brother might still be here.'

'Get him,' the doctor ordered. 'We need someone who knows him.' The nurse turned to the phone on the bedside table, moving an untouched jug of water.

'No, no!' said the soldier slightly too loud. 'It's not a Zulu. Dash, Dash Dot - Space - Dot. Golf Echo.'

'M-A-Y G-E-T,' spelt the doctor now completely confused. He looked at the Soldier who shrugged.

'Get me may.' said the nurse quietly. She looked at the Doctor who was none-the-wiser. 'I think it's a name,' she said. 'Get me May.'

'Who the fuck's May?' Everyone shrugged. The soldier continued to watch his eyes. His soldier's instinct told him to hold fire. Not to translate.

Dark brooding clouds came in beneath the radar and opened their bomb-bay doors over the leafy part of town. Beneath, some with brollies raised in defence, the mourners killed time. A few smiled at the rain, knowing it was in tune with his sense of humour. Many had stood around waiting for a pub to open, but for a crematorium, it was a first. There were a few nods from the old soldiers who recognised faces but struggled with the names. A few either didn't know or chose to ignore the request not to wear black.

When the doors opened, they filed in, grateful to be out of the rain but trying not to show it. Last in, the only man in uniform was the young soldier. No longer required to translate the code. With him walking in slow time was the nurse. People found seats awkwardly, shuffling along the narrow pews to make extra room. In a separate area sat the family, even in death we can't avoid ranks.

The coffin sat in a semi-circle of a curtain rail, the curtains open, revealing the coffin draped with a union flag and the dress hat of the dead man. A bottle of whiskey stood guard at the foot of the coffin. Outside, the brief storm whipped up the decaying orange leaves, brought to life by the wind, flipping them around the trees and the gravestones. A man in tails and a top hat closed the doors and entered a room off to the side. A bugle burst out and echoed around the high timbers of the crematorium, the sound slightly tinny through the speakers. The Last Post. A lady dressed in a suit started to speak. Few people noticed the door open, although the soldier and nurse felt the wind intrude where they stood aside from the pews. A woman entered, her hair pasted to her face by the rain, her face red as if from exertion. She wore a brightly coloured coat and highly polished boots, but she stood flustered and uncertain. The soldier looked at her. His eyebrows arched.

'You must be May?' he said to the woman.

She gave a start looking more frightened and confused. He looked at her hand. There was a faint mark of white, a band around the darker skin of her finger. The ring finger of her left hand bereft a ring. She nodded.

'He loved you very much,' said the soldier, locking his eyes with the woman. He could see the tears building up behind the will. 'Before he died,' he continued, 'he told me.'

The nurse looked at the woman, tears joining the rain on her face. 'And nobody knew.'

On Top Of The World

By
Joseph Phillips

The clouds cling to the mountainside, leaving above them a perfect ring of bare rock, free from the snow coating the lower slopes. Just inside the ring sits a lonely house, a solid stone construction hewn from the cliffs behind it. A gently winding path worn into the earth snakes down into the clouds, and into the chill wastes below. A stocky, muffled figure emerges from the house and proceeds to trudge through the thick mists.

Several hours later, the person reaches the valley floor, stops at the edge of a foaming river and dropping to their knees fills a waterskin. Pulling back some of the layers of cloth on their face reveals cold-chapped lips, they take a swig.

A small deer steps from a thicket of weedy saplings on the opposite bank, some two hundred metres from the kneeling figure. Both freeze instantly.

The deer pauses, sniffs the air, and turns its back.

Slowly, the hooded figure reaches into its pack and draws out a decrepit crossbow, worn with age and creaking, and a handful of carefully sheathed bolts. Quickly and quietly, one was nocked and aimed at the unknowing creature; a gentle squeeze and it is in the deer's chest. The animal staggers a few feet before it falls.

Dropping the bow, the person sprints to the stricken animal, pulling a foot-long knife from its belt as they run. The figure struggles to subdue the flailing deer; one of its hooves connects with their face. At last, managing to get the knife to its neck, slides the blade in at its collarbone. The deer's sides stop quivering and come to rest. The figure, panting from the sprint, pulls back its hood and the cloth around its mouth, revealing itself to be a woman, fifty-something with greying hair and dull hazel eyes, her cheeks and nose ruddy with the cold and exertion of running. A thin trickle of blood runs from where the deer struck her nose and pools at the corner of her mouth. She rests for a moment, glancing about for wolves and bears; then sniffs gruffly and proceeds to heft the carcass onto her shoulders. It starts to rain.

The mountain air is crisp, cold, and clean. The woman, Kendra, has lugged the deer back up to the hut above the snowline. Skinny from the past winter, the carcass is placed outside the hut's door while she goes inside, its legs sticking out from the body like a child's discarded toy.

She re-emerges from her house, knife in hand, and proceeds to gut the corpse slitting the stomach from chest to genitals. The intestines, crop, lungs, heart and other unnamed viscera slide partway out and have to be cut out the rest of the way, sagging to the slate gravel like a bin-liner of old clothes. Kendra pauses in her work. She glances at an almost imperceptible rise in the ground a few metres away, surmounted with a polished headstone, and tears fall.

Smoke curled from behind a ridge that stretched down from its mother peak like the arm of a fallen titan. Kendra peered over the top at the newcomers who had built it.

These new wanderers concerned her. Others like them had passed through her valley before but always moved on after a few days. This new group had roamed across the floodplain for over a week now, leaving hacked and burnt vegetation and a string of half-eaten carcasses in their wake.

Below her, five hide tents had been erected in a ring forty feet across, with the crackling bonfire at the centre, half a mile from the river. A few dozen people, mostly men, sat or squatted around it. A chunk of poorly-cooked meat in one hand and rough earth cup in the other. Dark brown liquid sloshed over the rims as their holders gesticulated wildly. Kendra noted that only the men were laughing; the few women present sat quietly, plastering a half-hearted smile on their face when the men pulled them forcefully into drunken embraces.

One man seemed calmer than the others, resting against a smooth boulder dragged into the range of the fire's heat. He lounged against his seat, naked to the waist and showing a muscular torso; he occasionally sipped from his cup. Another woman rested against his shoulder, strangely at ease in his presence, one arm draped over his chest.

A rumbling growl off to her right made Kendra look up from the revellers. Three large, bedraggled dogs tethered to a stake driven deep into the ground had caught her scent; the mountain wind had changed while she was distracted. They were large, unpleasant creatures, all matted grey fur and hanging jowls. They sat upright, each grizzled head facing her, drool dropping like rope from their jaws.

She looked back to the drunken mess of humanity below; they had not noticed her yet, but soon the dogs' nerves would break. She decided to give them a warning before that could happen. She tilted away from them, slipped out her crossbow and started to nock a bolt. The worn bowstring creaked as she pulled it back into the firing position. In one swift movement, she rose, and fired into the blaze, sending up a spray of sparks and scattering the logs.

'Leave this place!'

The group as a whole jumped back and froze at the sudden intrusion; it was five seconds before any of them thought to act. They cast around wildly, searching for the bolt's origin. One of the men took up a spear from its spot resting against a tent and threw it in vain in her direction, but he was too far out of range.

As Kendra started to leave, she couldn't get the image from her head of the calm man, the leader. After his initial surprise, he had simply stared at her as his fellows ran about frantically searching for bows and spears; an amused smile had played across his lips. But more disturbing had been the tiny girl peering out from behind the boulder, a collar around her neck.

The dogs were baying now, straining against the tough leather straps that held them. Kendra broke into a run, trying to put distance between her and the invaders before they could organise themselves. Harsh cries echoed out from behind the ridge, mingling with the howls of the dogs. She headed for the river; the dying light would slow them down, if she couldn't hide her scent soon the dogs would have her.

She made her way by memory as much as sight in the dying sun, looking back as she reached the edge of the rushing water. The ridge was swarming with torch-lit figures now, and as she watched, three shapes broke off from the glow of the torches. Kendra strode headlong into the freezing river following it downstream before stumbling into the deeper water at the heart of the current. Stinging water filled her nose and mouth for a moment before she surfaced. She splashed for the bank, staggered behind a mossy hillock and collapsed against it, still panting.

Kendra stayed still, waiting for a degree of warmth to seep back into her clothes until she heard a loud splash from the river. She froze, listening to the sound as it changed from the spattering of water on stone to the wheezing of a tired animal. The dog rounded the rock pile and stared aimlessly off into the darkness. Kendra drew her knife from where it nestled at her belt. As she stood, a single pebble slid out from under her foot. In an instant, the dog was facing her, its slab of a tongue lolling madly against dull yellow teeth. Two milky orbs gazed accusingly from the mass of flesh and fur, daring her to move.

They waited for an eternity crammed into a second before moving as one. The dog's clumsy lunge met only air as Kendra slipped past and slashed at the hound's back legs. The knife connected easily and severed a tendon; the dog crashed to the ground as its weight caused it to buckle. It tried hopelessly to turn and face her but fell with every attempt. Eventually, it stopped struggling; its eyes seemed mournful now, begging silently as she ended its life with a stab to the base of the skull. The giant head dropped against the shingle.

'Stupid creature.'

Kendra waited to regain her breath again before wiping the knife on the dog's fur. Only then did she turn in the direction of her hut.

Eight days after she revealed herself, Kendra was nearing the mountain path in the grey light of pre-dawn. Out of breath from the trek, she slumped against a lichen-encrusted tree. Looking down, Kendra noticed a protruding white growth of mushrooms. Lowering to her knees, she started to peel the soft fungi from the bark.

Suddenly, she heard muffled shouting a few hundred feet from her. She crept towards the source of the noise, a few scattered boulders way down the slope. It was one of the New Men, holding the tip of a spear to the throat of a woman pressed against a boulder, with the little-collared girl cowering behind her. The man started shouting in his harsh language, pointing at the girl with his free hand. The woman was on the verge of tears, shaking her head in desperation, pleading with him.

Kendra moved from behind a rock, directly behind the man with the sun at her back. The little girl didn't react, but the woman's eyes widened as Kendra drew her knife. Her captor saw it, turned and muttered something in his language. He stayed still, tense. The woman shouted something. In slow motion, the man's face twisted with a snarl and drove the spear into the woman's neck as Kendra rushed at him. The knife took him between the shoulders. He dropped alongside the woman's corpse.

Kendra looked to the girl; she stared back. 'Are you alright?' she asked.

The girl stared at her. Kendra pointed to the girl's collar before removing it from her neck, revealing a ring of sores.

Kendra spun around as a blast of sound echoed out over the valley - the man was blowing on a crude horn pulled from his belt. Kendra kicked it from his hand and slammed his head against the ground. He dropped still, but already other horns answered from across the plateau, and hoarse shouts were drawing nearer. Kendra grabbed the girl's arm and ran for the path.

Up the slope, Kendra looked back to see half a dozen hunched figures scrambling to their fallen ally, along with their tall-standing leader. He knelt at the now dead man, rose and pointed in her direction.

Kendra reached the hut half an hour later with the full dawn, tailed at a distance by the invaders. She ushered the girl into the hut, motioning for her to stay hidden behind the bed. Taking up her crossbow and quiver, she knelt outside the door, aiming at the edge of the mists.

The first to step from the clouds fell with a bolt in his forehead, the second one through his thigh. The rest emerged too quickly for Kendra to reload. She stood and drew her knife.

The leader cut an imposing figure against the golden, sunlit blanket behind him. He walked forward slowly, making no move to draw a weapon or raise his hands until he stood twenty paces from her. He regarded her for a moment, a childish grin playing over his features. Slowly, one arm rose and pointed lazily to the hut. Kendra glanced over her shoulder; the girl was peering through the window. His lips formed carefully around the unfamiliar language:

'That is mine.'

Kendra drew herself up to her full height. 'No. Not anymore.'

He smiled again, glanced at the floor, and covered the gap between them. A massive fist aimed at the space where Kendra's head had been a second before. She stepped aside, cut at his ribs and kicked his legs from under him. The giant toppled to astonished cries from his inferiors but rolled before she could press home her advantage. He was frowning now, confused. Watching the blade, the leader rushed at her, reaching out he grabbed her by the arm. He squeezed until she dropped the knife then threw her down like a discarded toy.

Kendra gasped as pain shot up her leg; she scrabbled in the dirt for her knife finding only stones. The leader loomed over her.

'No!' shouts the girl. His face contorted with the hideous smile again as he stretched an arm out to her.

A stone strikes him in the temple, and he falls. The remaining runts trip over each other in their scramble to escape. As they vanish into the cloud once more, the girl runs to Kendra and hugs at her legs.

Tears well in her eyes.

The Snow

By
Isabella Blackburn

I stood on top of the mountain leaning on my ski poles, my goggles around my neck and my hat pulled down tight over my ears. I looked down past the waves of the slopes to the small town, far away at the bottom of the valley. Around me, peaks pointed against the perfect sharpness of the winter sky. I was alone with the sounds were the breeze whistling and the constant hum of the ski lift some way behind me.

Shadows spread across the snow; the sun would sink behind the mountains soon. Far below, miniature people skied away or headed for the cable car down to the town. It was so clear, so beautiful. Behind me to the right was a deep dip holding a lake. It had a ring of cross-country skiers' tracks around the edge, a perfect circle with a row of glaciers hugging it. This was one of my favourite places, and I came as often as I could. I would ride the chairlift that rose past the lake and ended at the furthest, highest point of the resort. I wasn't supposed to go up alone, but the lift attendant knew me and let me on. Some days I would go up several times. He would always have a smile for me.

'Hello there, Kit, trying to set a record? How old are you this time?'

I would smile back and say 'Still nine and three quarters. It will be ten next time.'

I had to go home. I took a last, long look around then closed my eyes and imagined that I was as strong as this mountain. I put my goggles on and pushed off. The wind tore past like grasping hands as I sped down the slope, skis biting into the snow with each turn. Trees flashed by, a blurred kaleidoscope. I veered away from the marked run and took a path through the forest which would lead to my front door. The trees closed in as the path narrowed and I slowed down to duck under branches dressed in snow. My house was near the slopes; the cable car almost went over the roof. As I reached the treeline, I stopped by the biggest pine, took my glove off and stroked its rough, cold bark. This tree was my friend, and I imagined there was a heart beating slowly under the hard, wrinkly skin. Looking up I could see my treehouse, more of a platform than a house but it was mine. From here I could see the back of my house. It looked like it had been buried, the snow was heavy on the steep roof and the garage.

The garden had disappeared under metres of uniform white that rose taller than me. From the front, the house looked taller than it was. It looked dark, and my tummy tightened as I saw the empty driveway. I leaned on my tree and smelled its clean sharp scent. My father always said it was scent not perfume. I knew that I was very lucky to have this life, people kept telling me that. But coming up to my front door I had to remind myself to breathe. I put my skis away in the garage and knocked the snow off my boots by kicking the wall by the front door. The gaps in the ski rack showed that my elder sister was away on a skiing expedition with her school. The empty space on the driveway was where my father's car should be, my mothers' Beetle was in the garage. My older brother was at boarding school, so that left just me – and Her.

Boots off, I stepped quietly into the hallway. Daylight was fading fast, and no lights were on. I could see the flicker of flames from the fireplace through the living room door. As I took off my jacket and ski pants I glanced down the stairs to the left, to my parents' room, it was dark too. The house was silent. I slid into the living room and saw that my mother was sitting in the armchair by the fire, the flames made moving shadows on her face.

'I'm back.'

She looked at me, her eyes blurry dark pools. Her short dark hair was a mess; her face looked puffy and red. She had been beautiful once. I had seen photos of her looking happy, her black hair long, eyes dark and clear. She had looked exotic. Not anymore. An empty bottle and wine glass stood on the table by the chair. She didn't say anything, just stared at me as I stood in front of her. My cheeks tingled, and my breath stuttered.

'How are you?' I asked. 'Have you had a good day?' Stupid questions really, considering.

'He's not coming back you know.' Her voice slurred out the words, low and vicious. 'He's gone, and it's your fault he's not coming back.'

She meant my father. He had gone on a business trip, at least that was what I had been told. He would come back; I was almost sure that he would.

She was waiting for a reaction, watching me, squinting through the folds of her face. A poisonous toad squatting in the armchair. I kept my face still and said nothing. Breathed deep, felt the strength of the mountain. I am a mountain; I feel nothing.

'Did you hear what I said? He won't come back. He can't stand the sight of you.'

I stood still, watched the flames dancing, looked at her again. She was still waiting for me to say something or do something. She wanted a result. I wouldn't give her one. I thought about leaving her in the chair, stewing in her misery. I switched on the standing lamp behind her, and she flinched at the light.

'Have you eaten anything?' I asked. I wondered if there was any food.

My father had been gone for a few days, and I didn't think she had been out. We were far up the mountain and there were no shops within walking distance. She would only have gone if she had run out of wine. She wasn't safe in a car. I shuddered when I thought of the last time we had been in her car. My friend John had come to play, and his mother had said that he had to be driven home. He'd insisted even when I tried to tell him it wasn't a good idea. My mother had almost driven us off the road. I made her stop at the top of the hill and told John he had to walk home from there. Getting back to his was so scary. I had to keep my hand on the wheel steering for her, and even then, we were all over the place. Lucky for us that it was so quiet up here. John had probably told his mother, I didn't think he would come to play again.

In the kitchen, I had a look in the fridge, milk, some cheese, a couple of eggs. Nothing easy. I hadn't learned to cook anything much. My sister was good at cakes and in one of her sober moments my mother had taught me to make béchamel, but that wasn't much use now. I found a jar of pickles and had a couple while I searched for something else. There was some bread that wasn't too stale; I sliced it, the pieces uneven and ragged. Cheese and toast would do. I took the plate through, held it out to her. Her hand smacked into the plate, knocking it out of my hand. I watched it fly across the room and crash into the quiet.

'I don't want your disgusting food. You are a waste, useless, good for nothing. Nobody loves you.'

'Maybe you should go to bed.' I kept my voice low and even, polite. Pleased that it didn't tremble. 'It's getting late.'

She reached for the wine tried to pour nothing into the glass.

I took a deep breath. 'Maybe you have had enough?' I waited, ready to duck, but looking at her I thought that she couldn't have reached me if she tried. I had gotten it wrong before though; she was unpredictable and could sometimes move really fast. I had learned the hard way that slow and quiet was best.

I stood and reached for her arm. 'It's time to go to bed now.'

She would start crying in a minute; I could see the look, I knew how this would go. First, she was horrible and then she would get sad. I pulled her and she let me help her. As she stood she staggered and it took all my strength to hold her upright, she wasn't a small person. We shuffled towards the stairs, and it was so hard not to let her fall. We made it to the bedroom; she tumbled across the bed. I took off her shoes and put a blanket over her. She would pass out now.

I went back to the living room and sat on the sofa, avoiding her armchair. I watched the flames, trying not to cry. I couldn't breathe, my throat burned and my hands were shaking. I hugged my knees tightly, tried to breathe like I could on the mountain. I wouldn't let her win; she would not beat me down. I scrubbed my eyes, swallowed. I picked up the mess on the floor and threw it away with the wine bottle. There were two more already in the bin.

Walking upstairs I turned the lights on. The darkness was scary, and I had a system. The lights downstairs would have to go off, so I would run and switched the upstairs ones on first, then go down, turn off the bottom lights, and run up again without looking back. I cheated and left the bathroom light on. I would get yelled at if anyone found out, but she was asleep, so it would be ok. I snuggled in my bed with Lefky. I rubbed his worn-out fur and rubbed his silky ear on my lips. I had one of my mothers' Mills and Boons, but I didn't want to read.

My sister was due back tomorrow evening. I was sure my father would be soon too. He said he wouldn't be gone long. They would come back, and my mother would become a wonderful, normal person. She would tell my father how difficult I had been while he was away, how she didn't know what to do with me and I would stay quiet.

I lay in bed and thought about trying to tell him how Mum was when there was no one to see. I could ask him if it was my fault, if the things she said were true, maybe that was why he kept leaving. I could tell my sister. They knew she liked to drink. It was a game, hiding the wine, only letting her have two glasses. But she was very good at lying; I had seen it lots of times. She had a way of making people believe her and I wasn't nearly as clever. I hugged my knees, tried to think of what to do.

My window glowed, and I stood up on my bed and opened the window. The moon was calling me. A blast of freezing air swirled around me. I grabbed the ledge, lifting myself out onto the roof of the garage, pulling the window shut behind me. The back of the house was shorter than the front. It was easy to reach the ground, just a short slide into the snow. I stood in the driveway in my knee-length flannel nightgown, feet bare. I could have used the front door, but this felt more like an escape.

The moon lit everything in dark blues and glowing whites. White on white on white. I walked away from the drive onto the lane leading down the hill as the chill rose up my bare legs. Each foot landed soundlessly in front of the other; I left no trail behind me. I am Nobody, a ghost in the air. Trees lined the edge of the lane, dark guardians in ermine coats; my tree was the leader. The lane was a silver rope buried in soft powdery flesh. A pale scar in perfection. My feet had gone numb, my body belonged to the snow. I was the snow, freezing, unfeeling. The moonlight glowed, and when I looked at my hands, they were white. I reached the curve in the lane and stopped. I turned to look at the house. It stood, a bulky dark blot looming over me.

I could turn away and keep walking, never go back. No one would know where I had gone; it would all go away, I would go away, disappear into the forest. Walk up the mountain to the lake and sit in its perfect circle, protected by the glaciers. And she would have won, she would have beaten me, and I would be lost. Slowly my feet began the return, back up the hill, into the driveway, up the snow bank, onto the roof and through the window. I lowered myself into the room, latched the window and drew the curtain. I crept under my duvet, numb.

I was somebody.

Arsenic Annie

By
Ivy Ivison

'Oh, don't be afraid of my cakes, dear.' Now, this sentence uttered by any other old woman wouldn't stir an uneasy emotion within the gut. But the fact it's uttered by Arsenic Annie, the very woman who fed the same cake to three of her grandchildren and let them fade to nothing before her eyes is why I'm not leaping at the opportunity of a Victoria sponge. Though it deeply saddens me since that is my favourite cake. For a woman who does such dark deeds, you'd think her house and appearance would match. Instead, she's a flurry of peacock blue and green, her home clashing in a mix of burnt orange and eye-blinding yellow. It puts my drab slacks to shame, but I choose not to dwell on that for now.

'I'm not afraid, Mrs Bowen, simply full to the brim from lunch.' I place my hand on my stomach, shoving it out the best I can and pull what I hope is the generic *'I'm full to burst'* face. 'I think a cake of such loveliness would be best enjoyed when one isn't nearly bursting the button of their trousers. I will have to politely decline at this moment in time.'

That receives a sharp chortle. It's not a laugh, a guffaw or even a snort. It's this hollow thing all adults gain at precisely the age of thirty, and it sounds just as dead as they are on the inside.

'Such manners, your mother would be quite proud,' said Mrs Bowen.

She wouldn't since she hates me and is now dead, but I digress.

'Maybe I can wrap up a slice for you to take home for later, don't want you to miss out that's all.' This is a fight a young man cannot easily win. Old ladies are like drug pushers, relentless in nature but have a soft preen about it that makes it less terrifying than if it were a long-coated fellow pulling out a little sack of white powder from his pocket and trying to lure me into a dark alley to buy it. Though Arsenic Annie quite enjoys a different form of white powder.

Oh, I should probably tell you why I'm in such a peculiar situation. I seem to attract homicidal people. I don't mean to or want to, and yet I tend to wind up within their charming company. What about me draws them in? Haven't the foggiest. If I did, I certainly would have done something to stop it many moons ago. Instead, I've paired up with a local police officer with a moustache that Inspector Clouseau would turn green with envy over. How does one discover that they are a murder magnet? It involves a mixture of one dash of three-year-old innocent me, a sprinkling of a homicidal librarian, crack in one corpse and stir vigorously with confusion and dumb luck. Bake for seventeen years and hey presto. Speaking of baking, we should focus back on Arsenic Annie.

'Are you alright dear? You don't seem to be talking much today. Not ill, are you?' Though her question seems one of concern via the wording, the glint in her eye provides a darker twist.

'Oh, I'm perfectly fine, Mrs Bowen. You know what it's like when you overeat. I'm probably just sleepy. Enough about me, how are you today?' Stroke the ego of the sociopath, it makes them purr.

'Little old me?' She lets out another one of those decayed inside laughs and places a hand on her chest. Maybe she's playing coy, but I don't care for those being murdered enough to flirt with a grandmother. A man must have lines he does not cross.

'Well, I baked cakes as you know.' she gestures to the cakes littering the table; my mind makes them look rotten, so they're less appealing.

'Speaking of cakes, care to divulge any recipes? I've never partaken in baking before, hearing from quite a talented cake maker would surely help me with that.'

Mrs Bowen practically beams, leaning across her startling orange armchair to place her liver-spotted hand on my knee. I try not to cringe back into my chair, though I do momentarily imagine the sweet release of being swallowed by the fabric.

'Well you see dear, I follow the basics. Eggs, butter, sugar etcetera. But then...' Her wrinkly lips, stained with a prune colour lipstick decide to form quite the stomach-churning smirk. Who knew old ladies could be so unsettling?

'But then?' Maybe my patience is not the best but would yours be in this situation? I can tell my prompting wasn't met with great vigour since she seems to lean back a little. I'd ruined her dramatic pause, not the best decision in my life but alas I can't rewind time sadly, though it would be a far better power then attracting sociopaths.

'Enough about cakes, dear. I invited you here for condolences. I am terribly sorry about your mother. Such a shame.'

I'm not a fan of being touched, nor am I a fan of being touched emotionally and yet here I sit having an old wrinkled murderer trying to do both. A tight smile is all I can do as her hand rubs my knee.

Let's get this out of the way, shall we? My mother stole a Colt Model 1862 Police Percussion Revolver from her current lover, blasted from her phonograph the sweet music of Orpheus in the Underworld Overture and just as it hit the last few notes…She shot herself in the forehead. She was always so dramatic. Once a theatre performer, always a theatre performer.

Moving on, Arsenic Annie pauses awaiting a reply to her condolences. After hearing so many it's hard not to snap, but one must keep composure if they wish to maintain the underlining of respect in their name. Or something along those lines.

'Why thank you, Mrs Bowen. I'm sure she would have enjoyed your company and your cakes.' That brings back the discomforting smile from earlier, but there's a slight twitch to it before she tries softening her look. It doesn't work. If anything, it makes her more frightening.

'If only I knew whether you enjoyed them or not.'

I resist the urge to place my hand upon my chest to cover the slight wound from her verbal shot. Before a reply is made she begins to rise, a slight struggle to it which has me rise myself and offer a hand. As she takes it, her skin is as cold as her victims when she's done with them, but I manage to clamp down on any unsavoury reactions.

'Care to join me in the kitchen?' She sweeps her hand to the left of her, the open archway looking into quite the ugly kitchen.

Considering her living room is a vibrant cacophony of sun bright colours, the kitchen looks as if all life has been sucked out of it. She doesn't let go of my hand, unfortunately, expecting my guidance toward a room she quite obviously can reach on her own. Tucking her arm under my own, we make our way to the dreary room. An immature thought passes my mind in which I wonder whether she not only drains the life out of her grandchildren but also tortures her kitchen in similar ways. I'd probably look exactly the same, with peeling wallpaper and long since faded colours, if I had been stuck in her company for so many hours.

'What a marvellous cast iron stove you have, Mrs Bowen.' It is far from marvellous; it's a great big hulk of a black iron monster. The stove is something a child would dream up within a very dark nightmare and imagine being shoved into. Hansel and Gretel beware.

'She's one of my greatest treasures.' Her eyes glaze over with a fogged awe at the monster, and she lets go of my hand to press them against the side of it fondly.

Well, we at least know she's capable of love. Annie suddenly lets out the very *ah* that many have within a eureka moment. To say I nearly leapt from my breaches is an understatement. Her index finger is raised to the sky, and she turns pointing it at me. Noticing the paling of my pallor, something I wish I could help, she lets out a giggle.

'Oh, dear did I frighten you? My apologies. See I have just thought of something I could give to you to help with your grief. I'll be back momentarily, make yourself at home.' Making myself at home is the last thing I want to do, no thank you, Mrs Bowen.

'Frighten? No, possibly a slight startle.' My joking tone causes her to widen her smile, and I have seen many a taxidermy cat in mid-hiss that look far more inviting than the toothy grin presented to me at this moment in time.

'Honestly, Mrs Bowen, you do not have to give me a thing. Your condolences and company are all I need at this trying time.' She waves her hand at me as if to dismiss my words and heads back into the living room.

While snooping is awfully rude, it can be forgiven when it's to find evidence of a murder. The cupboards are standard, filled with different baking sugars, I do take a moment to lick my finger and stick it in the container to taste. Detective Henderson would turn his gaze to the sky asking a higher power for patience if he were witnessing this. The image of him doing so brings some amusement to this situation. There's also tins of unknown meats and the occasional rat dropping within the cupboard. Not a single murder weapon to be found within here, unfortunately. I check the stove, opening a few doors to check for children Annie has shoved inside, but there are no roasting toddlers to be seen. Not to say I haven't witnessed such things before, but that story is for a different day. The fridge, however, upon opening it I'm greeted by a foot. Yes. A foot. Bile rises in my throat not from seeing a foot, you'd be surprised how often I see dismembered body parts, but the nausea is caused by the fact this foot is at least a month old. Needing a momentary break from the smell, I shut the door and Arsenic Annie being in the doorway looking positively annoyed at my snooping is not a sight I wanted to see.

A grandmother is good at two things, complaining about her joints and overfeeding whichever family member decides to visit. Annie has another; she can grab a butcher's knife far too quickly for someone of her age. As she moves forward, the butcher's knife shining with afternoon sun but not nearly as inviting, I realise my mistake. I come to this conclusion when I try to twist the backdoor knob, and the bloody thing resists me. Trapped in the corner, door to my side and the fridge removing any chance of me side-stepping her less than friendly advances, I do what any respectable gentlemen would do in my circumstances; I charge at her. My shoulder collides with her chin, and we both have gravity shoving us down onto the floor. Grandmothers do not make great landing pillows. Arsenic Annie's butcher knife skids across the floor and we both scramble to get a hold of it, but alas, she somehow beats me to it despite me knocking the air out of her. She stands on shaky legs, eyes reflecting on her knife as she points the sharp blade toward me. I rise slowly; hands held out on either side. Annie reaches behind her, opening the basement door and twitches her head back.

'Did your mother never teach you not to snoop?'

Actually, she didn't teach me a damn thing. Taking a deep breath, I stand a little straighter, and my anger pulls my muscles taught.

'No, did your mother ever teach you not to poison your grandchildren?'

Well, that brought a new shade of red to Annie's

face, and she wastes little time as she lifts the knife above her head. A knee-jerk reaction kicks in; my leg is rising before I can even think of how to handle the situation and soon my black brogue connects with Annie's torso.

I never believed people when they said time slows down during such situations but the way Annie tumbled down the stairs into the basement felt far more stretched out than it should have. My eyes follow her, my ears pick up every crack of bone as she hits each step until a thud lets me know she has reached the bottom. Stepping forward slowly, I looked down into the dark; I can hear nothing but sirens blaring within my head. Or are they outside of my head. There's a blur to my vision and a shaking to my shoulders. I've never killed another human being but here I stand, Annie's empty gaze looking up from the bottom of the staircase and I wonder if I am now no better than she is.

'Nathaniel? Are you alright?' Detective Henderson with his moustache cleanly presented as ever, grips my shoulders tight but they still shake. He's breathing heavy, and the back door is now lying in pieces on the floor.

When did they break down the door? Noticing he's still waiting for a reply, I open my mouth, and only four words rise from my shock.

'What have I done?'

View From The Hill

By
C J Mitchell

They stopped under the shade of a large sycamore as Julia grabbed Danny's arm for balance and wriggled a finger inside the back of her shoe. They were still half a mile from their destination at the top of the hill. A golden retriever trotted past them with its tongue lolling out the side of its mouth followed by its elderly owner who offered them a friendly smile. Julia nodded in reply and pulled her damp top away from her chest, trying to get some flow of air underneath. Danny gave a wave and smiled at the dog now several meters ahead. He passed the bottle of cider he was holding to Julia who gulped down a few mouthfuls for some cold relief.

They finally got together during their last year at University after first meeting at a social during Freshers. Julia had studied photography and Danny journalism. After graduation, they moved in together to a small two-bedroom terraced house on the North side of town.

Long enough now for habits to show through the fine cracks of the initial charade of perfection. Julia had noticed Danny leaving the bathroom door open as he sat on the toilet. Then there were mealtimes where he would suck air into his mouth and let the food dance around inside until it was cool enough to swallow. She wasn't without her own faults though. She would not admit to leaving a single piece of toilet paper on the roll without changing it or her dirty cup and plates by the side of the sink.

Julia was walking up the hill with Danny as it had been a year since his Mother had died after a short battle with cancer and her ashes had been scattered there. Despite living in the town for four years, Julia had never been to the top, either by car or walking. In fact, she barely walked anywhere these days since passing her licence. She had asked if she could drive and park at the nearest carpark instead of down in the village, at least then she could have had the air-conditioning on and wouldn't be sweating like an amateur runner trying to do a marathon.

'Not far now,' Danny said as he walked in easy strides. Over a foot taller than her his longer legs seemed to barely feel the strain of the increasing steepness of the slope. Julia slipped every so often on the loose stones kicking up dust that covered her feet and made a tideline where her shoes met against bare skin. Danny shifted the backpack of food he had been carrying and slipped an arm around her waist.

'Come on,' he said. 'You're doing great. It'll be worth it when we get to the top.'

'Did your Mum use to walk up here?'

'We all did, Mum, Gran and Grandad. We'd bring the dogs up; they slept well after a walk up here.'

'I could do with some sleep now,' said Julia.

'You'll miss the view if you do.'

Julia looked up at the path ahead to where the crest of the hill appeared on the horizon that didn't seem to be getting any closer.

'I'm sleeping when we get back,' Julia said as they carried on. 'And next time we go anywhere I'm taking the car.'

'You sleep too much.' Danny sighed and began walking on ahead linking his thumbs under the straps of the backpack.

'Wait, what?' Julia forced herself into a slight jog to catch up. 'I don't sleep too much.'

'Made you walk a bit faster.' Danny grinned and nudged her. 'But you don't get out as much as you used to.'

The path seemed to grow steeper with every step she took and each step more painful as the back of her shoes continued to rub against her heels. She glanced back to where she had left her car and hoped it would be safe. The small red Fiat had been a graduation present from her parent's something they could at least agree on.

Two skylarks weaved overhead chirping at each as they flew high against the azure blue sky. She watched as Danny laid out a plaid woollen blanket beneath an oak tree and carefully arranged paper plates with various picnic foods. She picked up another bottle of cider, opened it and glugged down a few mouthfuls before selecting a mini pork pie and biting it in half.

'Could have waited till it was all ready.'

'I'm hungry after that walk,' she bit into the rest of the pie. 'Hope your Mum appreciates us coming all the way up here.'

'I thought you would when we reached the top.' Danny sat back against the trunk of the tree. 'Mum always did like you though.'

'Your mum liked everyone.'

'Yeah, she was the friendliest person I've known.'

Julia looked back down the hill at the route they had taken past hedgerows and fields and the path that wound back towards the stone houses of the village.

'It isn't much of a view,' she said sipping the cider.

'That's because the view isn't on this side,' Danny said as he picked up a ham sandwich. 'I'll show you after we've eaten.'

They sat eating mini scotch eggs, sausage rolls, and various sandwiches cut into neat little triangles. Julia shuffled under the shade of the oak tree and slipped her shoes off. Red marks showed where they met the back of her heels and she bemoaned having not thought of bringing any plasters or better walking shoes.

'How often did you used to come up here.'

'Since I was a little kid. Maybe once a month or more when the weather was nice.'

'Didn't you get bored?' asked Julia

'Not really. We always had a picnic like this, and I liked playing ball with the dogs. You know I think we should get one.'

'Get what?'

'A dog doesn't have to be a large one. Just…a dog.'

'Why do you want a dog?' she looked in the rucksack to see what was left amongst the empty packaging and found a box of French Fancies. 'You were hiding these.'

'A dog would be great. We could go out for walks together. Go to the park; it'd give us a great excuse to get out more.' He smiled at her.

Julia opened the box took out the plastic packet of cakes and looked at them. 'There's no chocolate ones.' she dropped the packet on the grass between them.

'You do know they all taste the same.' Danny said as he brushed crumbs off his top.

'I like the chocolate ones.'

'Sorry, I couldn't see through the box.' He picked up the packet and opened the plastic covering.

'Wait, we should have taken them back.'

'Why? I like them, doesn't matter which colour they are they're all the same.' He took out a yellow one and offered her the rest. 'So, shall we get a dog?'

'We're not getting a dog. They make too much mess and are a lot to look after.' Julia fanned herself with the empty French fancies box, leaving the cakes in their plastic casing on the grass, she stretched out her legs and closed her eyes.

'Don't fall asleep yet,' Danny nudged her. 'I still have to show you the view.'

'Can't we just go home now?'

'Not just yet.'

She waited as Danny packed away what was left of the picnic into the rucksack and stood up. The sun had moved from its highest point in the sky, but the rippling view of the distance showed its heat had not lessened. Julia's mouth felt dry, and her head was feeling fuzzy from the cider. As she stood she reached out to the tree to balance herself, and something crawled over her hand, she shrieked in terror and began hopping about rubbing her hand and stamping on the ground around her.

'What on earth?' asked Danny, laughing at her.

'A spider just crawled on me.'

'We are in the countryside.' He put the rucksack over one arm and offered a hand to her.

'This is why I hate going out,' Julia picked up her shoes and walked off barefooted on the dry grass.

'We get spiders in the house.' He trailed after her.

At least the ground was more level now and other than trees and a few bushes the landscape was open. She passed groups of yellow flowers that resembled daisies and clusters of tiny purple bluebells amongst grass faded to a dull brown. The dried earth kicked up in dust clouds around her feet. A slight breeze cooled her face, and she sucked in the refreshing air. She listened to the trill of birds and noticed the lack of car engines or lorries clanking with heavy loads as they did along the road where they lived. Taking her phone out of her trouser pocket she thumbed to the camera setting and snapped a picture of the flowers, she smiled and thought it would look better taken with her Canon SLR back at home. Flicking through her older pictures, she caught her footing, fell, and dropped the phone. Danny hurried to her side.

'Are you okay?'

'No, I fell over, and my ankle hurts,' she said clutching her ankle with tears in her eyes. 'I've dropped my phone, and I think I've broken it.'

'Can you stand up?'

'I don't know, it hurts,' she looked around herself for her phone and found it in arms reach. Picking it up, she saw the screen partly cracked showing a photo of them together at University.

'Well, that's typical.'

'It's okay, we'll get it fixed,' Danny said. 'Come on; it's not far now. We can't have come all this way for nothing.'

He reached out a hand to Julia and helped her up she clutched onto his arm and tried walking, but her ankle gave out causing her to wobble and almost fall again. She stopped and began crying.

'It hurts too much. I shouldn't have come out here.'

'We can sit down again once we get there,' he said. 'Come we're nearly there.' Danny put his arm around her waist, and she leaned on him wincing with every step. She wiped the tears from her eyes with the back of her hand while clutching her phone.

'I was taking a photo of the flowers,' she explained, as they made their way towards the edge of the hill.

'I haven't seen you do any photography for a while.'

'Guess I haven't been anywhere to do any.'

They reached the edge and sat on a metal bench facing outwards to the view, Danny sat her down carefully and joined her on the bench. The vista before them spread out for miles. A large mass of houses and buildings enveloped with squares of fields in yellows, greens, and browns with hedgerows and trees marking out the boundaries. In the distance was the greyed shadow of another hill that wrapped around the town below them.

'I didn't realise the town was so big.'

'It's grown since I first used to walk up here.' Danny pointed out some stone buildings to the left. 'It used to be just from there now it's about half as big again.'

She leaned her head on his shoulder and sat quietly for a while looking at the view trying to figure out which buildings were which. Some were obvious like the spires of churches and the taller towers. From here all the houses looked the same other than the various shades of their roofs. She watched a small group of sparrows flying overhead until they passed out of sight.

'You're right,' she said. 'It is a good view.'

'I'd take you to see more, but you can't always drive to places like this.'

'Alright, I get the hint,' she smiled and snuggled into him.

'We'll need to head home soon.'

'Just a little bit longer.'

They sat and watched as the sun made its way over the horizon and shadows began to cast across the town below. Together they stood up and held hands as they made the long walk back down the hill to the village where Julia had parked her car.

'Come on its stopped raining,' Julia said, as she attached a lead to Freddo's leather collar, picked up a few small black bags, and put the camera in her satchel. They had finally decided on a rescue springer spaniel after looking for several months for the perfect puppy. She left the house zipping up her blue raincoat and putting the satchel over a shoulder while holding Freddo's lead in her left hand. She walked him past her car parked in the driveway and as he began to tug towards the right she turned left to join the main road.

'Not our usual route today,' she said, as they continued walking. Leaves clogged the drains along the edge of the road and rainwater pooled amongst them like tiny urban ponds.

Her phone pinged in her pocket, and she looked at the message.

'Looks like Daddy is going to be a little late coming for a walk,' she smiled. 'Just you and me today Freddy.'

She looked along the road ahead of them and set a steady pace towards the hills in the distance.

Odile or no Odile?

By
Mark Webber

'I want the cheapest phone you've got,' I told the salesman. 'I don't need to surf the interweb or take photographs. I just want to make phone calls and send messages.'

I was in the Banana shop in the High Street (all right, it wasn't actually 'Banana'. I've changed the name to protect the guilty and deny them any undeserved publicity. But they're the people Jeanette Winterson mentioned when she decided that 'Bananas are not the only Fruit' wasn't a suitable title.

What was I even doing there? I hated mobile phones. (I still would if I hadn't decided to expunge the word 'hate' from my vocabulary.) As usual, it was a case of *Cherchez la femme.* I had fallen under the spell of a girl (and when I say 'girl', I mean no disrespect to the 45-year-old divorcee in question.) She was under a spell of her own. She was wedded to her phone and she couldn't understand why I didn't have one. Her ex was a *grand fromage* in one of the French mobile phone giants (I did say she was *Madame*, didn't I?) Every year, he gave their 14-year-old daughter a new I-phone and she, the dutiful daughter, passed the old one on to her mum, with whom she lived.

The Banana man produced a lilac-coloured number at £14. That seemed like a steal to me. It was the one that sounds like an Old Testament prophet exercising his vocal cords (Samsung – do try to keep up.) There was even a little credit-card-sized piece of plastic to top up the phone with. So with a cheery, 'Thanks, I was wondering what I could cram into the few microns of space left in the credit card compartment of my wallet' I bade him farewell. I was ready to step out into the Brave New World of 21st-century telephony. And my *Madame* was waiting.

I suppose that back in the spring of 2008, we must both have been lonely souls looking for the one who would make us complete. How else to explain that we met on an internet dating site? It didn't bill itself as such, and most people using it were blissfully unaware of its true nature. I was myself. I thought I'd signed up to a website for international pen friends, in line with my interest in languages and internationalism. It was strange. Members were supposed to use the internet to make contact, but after that, they were meant to correspond by snail-mail. There was nothing to pre-vent them from exchanging emails too (and no doubt many did).

I remained true to the spirit of the website. I responded punctually to anyone who contacted me, male or female, gay young thing (in the original sense of gay) or Downtonesque dowager (not too many of those contacted me, actually.) But if I responded more quickly to the younger female ones, can you find it in your hearts to blame me? After all, I was probably only unconsciously responding to the same instincts that motivated the caveman when he dragged his mate into the cave by the hair (not that I would endorse the behaviour of that erstwhile serial abuser. He didn't know any better whereas we would have no excuse for such appalling conduct.)

After the initial contact, Odile and I passed immediately to postal correspondence. She couldn't have made a stronger impression if she'd spent the previous six months researching my preferences (perhaps she had – creepy thought!) She wrote in black ink with a fountain pen (a big turn-on for a pen lover like me) and her handwriting was intriguing. The letters were well formed with well-developed upper and lower loops, indicating an open, sensuous nature, and overall her script was pleasing. I was optimistic about the content of her letters too. She sounded open-minded and eager to learn.

With her third letter, Odile sent some photographs of herself. I thought she must have sent pictures of her daughter by mistake. She didn't look much over 18. She had blonde hair cut into a fringe and an enigmatic, innocent-looking little smile.

Soon after that, impatient with the delays of conventional post, she suggested that we switch to emails. And then, she asked me to call her.

I was hesitant. Calling a strange, beguiling woman in a foreign country is not for the faint-hearted, even if she has invited you to (especially if she has!) And I am nothing if not faint-hearted. From somewhere, I found a bit of courage. I made the call. Now, although lacking the experience of telephoning mysterious foreign women, I was alive to the etiquette of those situations. I knew Debrett's would tell me that a gentleman should always address a mysterious foreign woman in her own language. Hitherto, we had conducted our correspondence in English. Her English was of A-level standard. I had passed O-level French forty years before, and my knowledge was rusty, in spite of desultory attempts to keep it up over the years. However, I managed to make myself understood with my *Bonjour, Odile. Je suis Mark. Comment ca va?* Before we switched to English.

She didn't just want to chat, as it happened. She was coming to London for the day on the *Eurostar* with her daughter.

'Will you come to London and meet me?' she asked.

'I don't think I can, really,' I said.

It wasn't the answer she wanted.

'Oh, I see,' she said curtly. And then she hung up.

I knew at once that I'd put my foot in it, big time. She obviously saw that as the brush off. The fact was, I did want to meet her, but the sudden invitation had pushed me right into my discomfort zone. I rang her straight back. She sounded annoyed, but with a substantial slice of humble quiche (it's like humble pie only even more humiliating) I won her round. We arranged to meet in London.

It was more by luck than judgement that I managed to meet them in St Pancras. I'd taken a borrowed mobile phone (I still hadn't visited the Banana shop at that point) but it ran out of battery too soon. So, I shuffled up and down the station concourse, among hordes of passengers, looking for a blonde woman with a teenage girl.

I knew Odile was going to be tall. But I didn't know how tall. In fact, she was almost as tall as me. (Once, later on, I said that to her. I got the look. All men know what it's like. It's the one you get when you've said the wrong thing. I suppose tall women feel self-conscious.) She wasn't quite as young-looking as her photos had suggested (old photos, maybe) but she was very attractive. In one word, she was statuesque (in a good way.) The problem, though, was her daughter Eloise (not her real name, but close. Truthfully, I can't remember what her name was.) She was very pale, very blonde (much more than her mother) and very quiet. I wondered if she quietly resented my presence on an outing that was meant as her treat, but she didn't show any signs of hostility. The problem was two-fold: finding something that she wanted to do and something she would eat. We never cracked the eating problem, though she did nibble on one or two things (though apart from the pallor, she seemed perfectly healthy on her Spartan regime.) As for the activity, we took her to Camden Market, at her request, and then I took them on a Thames boat trip. Stroke of genius, that!

After London, the rhythm of our communications increased. We'd already abandoned traditional correspondence in favour of the instant contact of emails. If I'd been out during the day, I would invariably find several messages waiting on my return. I'd send an immediate reply which would elicit one straight-away from her. And the entire evening would pass that way.

Early on, I'd come to think of Odile as a shy person. That's how she'd seemed in London too. But I soon realised she was a lot less shy than me. It wasn't just the rhythm of our communications that increased. They became much more intense too. And in that, I was definitely not the prime mover. No one as shy as me (yes, I really was the shy one in that budding relationship) could have steered our communications in the 'cheeky' direction they now took. I've tried to ignore national stereotypes over the years. But Odile seemed to be doing her best to convince me that the tired old stereotype of the naughty, naughty *mademoiselle* was in fact valid. I was bemused, not being overly confident of my appeal, at the way an attractive Frenchwoman was saying what she proposed to do when she was lying next to me. As we'd only spent a few hours together, and then not entirely alone, I wondered if her approach wasn't a bit premature. However, I was pleased by the attention.

Obviously we had to meet again soon. She invited me to come and stay with her. She lived in a compact, two-bed-room flat in a little dormitory town twenty minutes out of Paris. After a couple of decades of travelling around Europe, and even living abroad, I'd now sunk into a torpor that prevented me from getting up and going anywhere. But I knew I was going to have to make an effort or forever wonder what we might have become together. I was so completely smitten that I even dared to imagine that she might be 'The One'.

I flew to Paris. Odile met me at the airport. By then, I'd been to the Banana shop. With my shiny new Samsung, I contacted her in the arrivals lounge. The energy flying between us when we first met was tangible. It was almost as if we'd met in a previous life. We got the train back to her town. I was staying in a hotel for the first night because Eloise was still at home. She would be going off to stay with friends after that.

My ideal relationship would grow gradually as the couple spent time learning about one another over weeks or months. It's an organic thing with a natural progression that can't be hurried, like the plants that are forced in commercial hothouses. Odile preferred to skip the gradual learning phase. Perhaps she considered that the weeks we had spent zinging messages back and forth between us were enough introduction. At any rate, she put the 'hot' into hothouse. I was uneasy at that 'full-on' approach to getting to know someone, but finally reflecting on the well-tried injunction 'if you can't beat 'em, join 'em', I allowed myself to be drawn into that hothouse activity.

By the end of the week, we had agreed to spend Christmas, still three months away, at a little house that Odile owned in the south of France. Eloise would be in Marseille with her father.

Before that though, we were going to meet again. Odile was coming to stay with me for a week. Meanwhile, our daily communication resumed. And I noticed a side of Odile that pleased me less (to be truthful, I had noticed it already, in Paris and before.) She was distrustful, intensely jealous and highly critical. Her distrust arose in part from being let down by various men, including her husband. As she'd been unfaithful to him, as she freely admitted, I wondered if she was distrustful partly because she expected everyone to behave like her.

I saw her jealousy when she introduced me to a friend. I never met that friend in person, and there was never any likelihood that I would; I just communicated with her a handful of times online. I never saw a photograph of her and didn't know what she looked like. And I never heard her voice. Odile knew that, but that didn't stop her from uttering suspicious, reproachful remarks on the subject.

At the time of Odile's visit, I had the use of a friend's car, a splendid, spacious number with an automatic gearbox. I met her at Swindon railway station and then, for the whole of her stay, took her wherever she wanted to go. Her underlying critical nature surfaced occasionally; for example, when I couldn't immediately produce an adaptor for her heated hair tongs, without which she would not go out in the morning. But otherwise, we got on pretty much as before. And I was as completely smitten as ever.

I saw Odile off again at Swindon station. As she stood looking down at me through the open train door, I fancied I saw something other than the pure, unalloyed affection I hoped to see. In her wistful little smile; was there a trace of regret? Of did I imagine that retrospectively? Given the way things turned out, it probably wasn't just my imagination.

I couldn't wait for Odile to get home. I knew she would immediately zing off an email, and our frantic exchange of electronic *billets-doux* would recommence. When I'd heard nothing by the end of that day, I was concerned. When I still didn't hear anything all the next day, I became agitated. When she was still silent as the third day drew to a close, I could contain my anxiety no longer. I fired off an email asking if all was well.

Odile made me wait for a reply. When at last she got back to me, it was to say that she didn't want to see me anymore. I asked her why. She said she didn't feel she could trust me. She'd had it with men, apparently. From now on, she was going to put her trust in other women (did I say that she'd already had several same-sex relationships?). I could have said that I'd scarcely had enough time to prove that I was untrustworthy, in the handful of days that we'd spent together. Her decision to end our fledgeling relationship before it had even taken wing was based on prejudice arising from previous experiences with men. But what was the point? She wasn't even listening by then.

I was gutted, to use a visceral but highly expressive term. I'd been full of hope for that relationship, right to the end. I'd even dared to think that she might finally have been the ONE. She evidently saw me more as another one.

It took me months to get over Odile. And what slowed the process down more than ever was that every time I felt in my overcrowded pockets for a pen or some loose change or my wallet, my hand made contact with a hard, oblong object. When I drew it out, I saw that it was a lilac-coloured Samsung mobile phone for which I had no use. I did eventually start using it though, in a desultory fashion.

One day, many months later, when I was working in a summer language school, a young colleague inadvertently set the seal on that whole sorry business. I'd taken out the phone and was fiddling with it when he observed 'That's a girly phone!' I said 'Who cares?' But I was thinking 'If you only knew, mate. If you only knew.'

Honey Cake

By
Carol Hilton

Polly had kept her promise to Marula. At midnight she'd sneaked out of the hotel room and negotiated the uneven steps down to the beach then waded towards the large rock, feeling the sand slide under her feet, gasping as the cool froth tickled her legs. It'd felt like a baptism as she plunged through each foamy wave towards deeper water. Finally, exhausted, she'd floated on her back and waited for an answer. And waited. Eventually, she'd splashed back to shore, and slumped down on the beach, rubbing wet sand off her feet. She hadn't believed that a midnight swim would resolve a joyless marriage, but a tiny part of her had hoped. Shivering, she dried her short blonde hair, her wedding ring slipping about on her slim finger as she rubbed. She twisted the ring off her finger, as though uncorking a bottle. She'd got into the habit of removing her ring when deep in thought, irritating her husband, Greg, who would tap her hand if he caught her. The ring glowed in the moonlight; a piece of metal chaining her to a man she shouldn't have married.

This time she didn't replace the ring but instead jammed it in her pocket before making her way back to the hotel. Greg was snoring, worn out from his final night of beer and back-slapping at the bar. She slipped into bed and waited for the pink dawn to peep through the shutters, dreading the alarm clock signalling the start of their return to Pathos airport and from there, the flight to London; back to a house that she never thought of as home.

On the return flight, later that morning, Greg hadn't noticed her missing ring. Not even when she'd mopped up a wine spill, cringing at his hissed complaints about her 'clumsiness.' Greg didn't approve of drinking at lunchtime and had silently fumed to see Polly accepting the complimentary Merlot to accompany her rather shrunken cheese croissant.

Before landing, Greg had wandered up the aisle to the toilet, giving Polly an opportunity to stretch out her hand and examine it properly. She could see the indented skin that her wedding ring had covered for eight long years. A strange feeling of euphoria crept over her as Polly inspected the little band of rose-pink skin tingling with the promise of youth. It was as though she had finally slipped out of a pair of familiar handcuffs.

Greg, still sulking about her lunch-time wine when they'd landed at Gatwick, ignored her as they waited silently in the chatting crowd for their cases. Pleased to see his baggage arrive first, he'd grabbed his bags.

'I'll get the car, see you outside in ten,' he'd commanded, before marching off.

Polly's suitcase, with its jaunty pink ribbon, arrived in the next batch. She let the case trundle past, watching it continue on its indifferent circuit. Just like my life, she thought.

When her suitcase continued to present itself to her every three minutes, she started to feel hot prickles on her

neck, convinced that security would start speculating as to
whether she was some sort of terrorist. The only objects left
on the belt apart from her suitcase was a blue baby buggy
and a cardboard box, encased in strips of cellophane, like
a modern-day Egyptian Mummy. Her suitcase, the pram,
and Mummy continued revolving like unwanted prizes in
a low-budget game show. A security guard wandered in
Polly's direction, causing her to panic and grab her case.
She pulled it towards the exit looking for somewhere to sit
and think. About the ring. About everything.

As Polly pulled the case along, she gritted her teeth;
Greg would be muttering about the delay. Funny how I
never noticed his impatience when we dated, she thought.
He'd been all smiles and jokes when they'd first met at a
charity dinner held at Greg's golf club. The combination
of his 'club president' blazer and confident manner at the
dinner table had impressed her. She'd laughed at his jokes,
little realising that he used the same repertoire with all
the ladies. After two months of wining and dining, he'd
proposed marriage and Polly had gratefully accepted.
She shook her head once again at the folly of marrying so
quickly. Why hadn't she dated him more? Lived with him
first? Found out what he was really like?

She spotted an empty seat directly in front of a departures screen and sat down. There was a Qantas flight that
evening. Twenty-nine hours later she could be at Brisbane
airport, hugging her sister. She shut her eyes imagining
Jodie's warm arms and her large family's excited babble.

When Polly's sister Jodie had moved to Brisbane, it'd
felt to Polly as if a limb had been severed. Polly had remained behind in London to care for their mother, but now
she had died, there was no family left, apart from Greg.
Working as a ward sister at Brisbane's city hospital, Jodie had
persuaded Polly, also a nurse, to apply there as well, but
before Polly had sorted out her visa, Greg had entered her
life. The sisters had resorted to corresponding regularly;
Jodie sending reams of cheerful photos of barbeques and
family holidays. Polly eagerly devoured any news about

her Australian nephew and nieces, not having any children of her own. Greg, being fifteen years older than Polly, hadn't wanted the 'fuss and mess' of a baby, and Polly had reluctantly accepted his decision.

Polly shifted on the hard metal seat. She should have discussed children with him before the wedding. She had just presumed Greg would like a family but although he loved her, in his own way, he wanted was a house-keeper. Now that she was thirty-nine, her chances of a baby were slipping away. She glanced up as the departure board flashed; the Brisbane flight was 'boarding.' She sat there imagining the long flight to Dubai, followed by the final stage over Australia's sandy brown interior before touching down in the shimmering heat of Brisbane. Greg considered flying to Australia 'a waste of money,' persuading Polly that it would be too much for her to travel alone. To mollify her, he took her on his four golfing holidays each year.

Polly little suspected that this summer holiday would be any different from the others. Greg had selected Cyprus, attracted by a newly built golf course near Paphos. He'd stuck to his usual routine; golfing all day, while Polly explored the local area. Hot and tired from a day of golf, Greg would shovel his dinner down before joining his new-found companions at the bar, leaving Polly to return to their room to read.

It was by chance, on the last day of their holiday, that Polly, exploring Paphos, decided to take a short-cut through a dusty alley. While looking for a street sign, an archway leading into a shady courtyard caught her attention. A sea of tables, decked in red-checked tablecloths sat waiting for their customers. Outside the kitchen, a sleek black cat lay asleep on a cracked plaster window ledge, framed by a spray of cerise bougainvillaea. Charmed by the scene, she decided to take a photo for Jodie. She skirted the tables to get a better picture, unaware that someone was watching her.

'Hello lady. You want to eat?' A voice called out across the tables.

Polly peered into the shadows and could just make out a grey-haired lady in a black dress, sitting at a table.

Startled, Polly shook her head. 'Maybe later,' she ventured, backing out towards the alley.

Undeterred, the woman persisted. 'Some coffee, or cold drink? Yes? Very hot
today.'

Polly hesitated, not wanting to hurt her feelings. She nodded. 'Thank you. A coffee please?'

'Nai, of course. Come sit. Sit.' She offered her chair to Polly and bowed her head formally. 'I am Mrs Marula Charalambous Papadopolous, but…,' she flicked a vine leaf off the tablecloth, 'you must call me Marula.'

Polly nodded and sank down into a wicker chair; she looked around. A cool breeze rustled through the sprawling vine overhead; bunches of tiny pellet-green grapes peeked out through the canvas of lush green leaves. From the dark kitchen entrance, she could hear the clatter of pans and occasional good-humoured shout.

Marula emerged triumphantly bearing a red plastic tray. 'Ena Coffee. And I bring you my special honey cake. It will make you happy. You look… a little sad.'

'Do I?' Polly was surprised that it showed.

'Nai.'

Polly looked at the brown plate. The golden cake was glistening with honey. She cut a piece and chewed. Studded with walnuts and pistachios; it was unlike any cake Polly had tasted before.

Marula nodded encouragingly, 'Good? Greek honey. The secret? Wild Oregano. My sister Kristina's bees.'

Polly took a sip of coffee; it tasted robust, thick and deliciously smooth after the heat of the streets. 'Does she live nearby?' she asked.

Marula sat down next to Polly and launched into an entertaining description of her family, some of whom worked at the local market. Establishing that Polly hadn't been to it, Marula offered to take her after she'd finished her coffee.

'I have to go later. We need aubergines for tonight. I will introduce you to my cousins and my sister, Kristina,' she announced.

'I'd love that.' Polly smiled properly for the first time that week.

After the second slice of cake, Polly accompanied Marula around the noisy market, stopping every few minutes to meet cousins, two uncles, an aunt and Marula's sister Kristina who'd hugged Polly enthusiastically before presenting her with a jar of honey. They'd rested on a wooden bench under a large fig tree and drank traditional coffee served in cups that reminded Polly of a doll's tea set. Polly told Marula all about Jodie and her family.

'Australia? So far.' Marula shook her head sadly.

'I miss Jodie…so much.' Polly looked down at her cup.

'Why do you not go?' Marula asked.

Polly hesitated. She'd never told anyone about Greg. If she'd revealed her despair over his behaviour, it would suddenly become real, something she would need to deal with. Over the years she had become immune to his interruptions and little put-downs, telling herself that he was just 'Grumpy Greg.' But now, under the rustling leaves, as she talked about Greg, she could see her life reflected in Marula troubled face.

'This is not good.' Marula shook her head.

Polly shrugged. 'Aren't all marriages like this?'

'Not all. My Georgiou was kind to me,' Marula said gently.

'I don't know what to do.'

Marula looked at Polly. 'I think in your heart you do.' She stopped herself going any further, then her face brightened. 'Ha. I know. Aphrodite will help.'

'Aphrodite? She's not real, is she?'

'No. I mean you must bathe at Aphrodite's rock.' Marula sat back, pleased.

'What?' Polly was even more confused.

Marula explained about the old legend of Aphrodite.

The locals believed that the off-shore rock marked the birthplace of Aphrodite rising from the sea. Women who swam around it in the moonlight would find 'the answer.'

'And it's near here, along the coast road,' she finished triumphantly.

'By our hotel.' Polly nodded.

'Good. Good. Go tonight before you leave. She will help you get what you truly need.' Marula grabbed her hand. 'Promise me?'

Polly hugged her. 'Promise.' She picked up her bag. 'I must go before Greg gets back.'

Marula rummaged in her basket and pulled out a package. 'Cake. For your journey.'

'Thank you ...for everything.'

Polly stood up reluctantly steeling herself for another dinner with Greg; listening to his golfing anecdotes while watching food crumbs nestle in his beard. She was even more determined to go through with her midnight swim.

A stern reminder about 'unattended bags' interrupted Polly's thoughts. It had been an hour since she'd left the baggage hall. Greg would surely have gone home by now. She returned her attention to the racks of books in WH Smiths looking for two for the long flight ahead.

She glanced around the bookshop in a daze, still unable to believe what she was doing. One minute she'd been sitting on an airport seat staring miserably at the departures board, watching the Qantas flight flash 'boarding,' and the next she'd queued up and bought a ticket for the next flight. As she had paid for the ticket, she noticed the package of honey cake in her handbag, still neatly wrapped. She was determined that she wouldn't eat it until the time felt exactly right. Marula would have approved, she thought. She dug the boarding card into her pocket, feeling a small round object with her fingertips. The wedding ring. She pulled it out; grains of sand clung to it, reminding her of the dark swim the night before. Someone grabbed her arm, jolting her back to the bright lights of the terminal.

'What're you doing Polly?' Greg said. 'I'm double-parked.' He pulled her arm impatiently.

Polly rubbed the bare finger where her wedding ring had been; the bare finger of an independent woman. She stood up. 'I'm not going home.'

'What?' Greg looked confused.

'I'm going to see Jodie.'

Greg's eyes widened. 'Are you daft? Come on, move.'

Polly held up her bare hand and wiggled it.

'What that supposed to mean?'

'It means I'm taking a nice long holiday, all by myself.' Polly felt almost giddy.

Greg's eyes bulged. 'I leave you to collect one bloody case…and you turn crazy,' he spluttered.

'Yes, I'm crazy, crazy to have acted as your housekeeper for eight years without a thank-you. It never used to be like this. I don't know what's happened to you.' Polly picked up her bags.

'Are you having one of those mid-life crisis things?' Greg said.

'Maybe I'm having a mid-life epiphany.' Polly said. 'Do you even love me?' She stared at him, hoping even now that he would throw himself at her feet and beg her for another chance.

But Greg just nodded his head slowly. 'I get it. You want a cleaner,' he wagged his finger at her. 'Do you know how much they cost? We'll talk about it at home.'

'No Greg. You don't "get it".' Polly waved her boarding card. 'I'm going to Brisbane.'

'If you get on that plane, I, I….' His eyes started to mist slightly. He turned away to look at the departure board.

'I'll call you when I get there,' Polly said softly. 'But right now, I really need my family.'

She felt exhilarated, almost as if she was jumping over last night's moonlit waves at Aphrodite's rock. As she walked towards the security gate, she reached into her handbag, broke off a large piece of honey cake, and popped it in her mouth. It tasted of sunshine and freedom.

This collection of short stories has been produced in conjunction with Vineleaves Publishing. An independent publishing company dedicated to New Writers and helping them to publish and promote their work.

All the stories in this edition have been written by past and present students of The University of Gloucestershire (at the time of printing) as part of a competition.

Further information about Vineleaves Publishing can be found on our website.

www.vineleavespublishing.co.uk

Follow us @VLPublishing.com.

All enquiries to info@vineleavespublishing.com

Lightning Source UK Ltd.
Milton Keynes UK
UKOW01f2040260218
318515UK00001B/30/P